LAUGH ON FRIDAY

For Ann Elgar, the chance to work in a Swiss resort at Madame Menton's ski club is a golden opportunity. Luc Menton, her employer's son, makes her especially welcome and soon it is clear that his friendly affection is turning to love. But Ann is spellbound by the sophisticated French actor Paul Duret who makes no secret of his infatuation with her. The more Luc and Madame Menton warn her against Paul, the greater becomes her desire to be with him...

LAUGH ON FRIDAY

Laugh On Friday

by
Patricia Robins

Magna Large Print Books
Long Preston, North Yorkshire,
England.

British Library Cataloguing in Publication Data.

Robins, Patricia
    Laugh on Friday.

    A catalogue record for this book is
    available from the British Library

    ISBN 0-7505-0793-4

First published in Great Britain by Hurst & Blackett
Ltd., 1969

Copyright © 1969 by Patricia Robins

Published in Large Print August 1995 by arrangement with
Patricia Robins.

Magna Large Print is an imprint of
Library Magna Books Ltd.
Printed and bound in Great Britain by
T.J. Press (Padstow) Ltd., Cornwall, PL28 8RW.

Tel qui rit vendredi, dimanche pleurera
(French proverb)

1

'Oh, I'll never master this language!' Ann thought as she sat beside Luc Menton listening to him ordering the correct sized skis for her in the little sports shop in Aiguille.

But she was not really depressed by her inability to follow the rapid conversation in French. There was far too much else to fascinate and entrance her for her to be anything but wildly thrilled and excited.

'How lucky I am!' she thought as her young Swiss companion selected a suitable pair of wooden skis that were adequate for a beginner and being second-hand, were cheap enough for her to be able to afford from her meagre currency allowance. For a brief moment she felt sorry for Luc's younger brother, Pierre, who had gone to England in her place. No doubt it would be raining at home. February was always one of the most depressing months of the winter. How he must be missing this bright hot sunshine, the laughter, the fun that seemed to surround his home. Lucky Luc and Pierre to grow up in a place such as this even if they had had to go down to the valley to boarding school in the term time. All their holidays would have been spent here, half way up a Swiss mountain with ski-ing through the winter until Easter and then swimming, golf and wonderful mountain expeditions to make in the summer.

Ann Elgar's blue eyes crinkled in a mischievous grin. There was no doubt in her mind as to who had the better of the exchange bargain arranged between her mother and Madame Menton. He had the advantage of being able to take as much Swiss money over to England as his parents could allow him and live with her family as one of them. She had only been able to come here as a glorified au pair and would earn her pocket money helping Madame Menton run the little club where skiers congregated for drinks and sometimes lunch; for the daily tea-dance and at night for après ski entertainment.

Ann allowed herself the briefest of sighs. Madame Menton had told her mother

10

that it would not be suitable for a well-brought-up young girl to help in the club at night. Ann's services would only be required during the day and already she had learned from Pierre's twenty-two-year-old brother, Luc, that it was more fun in the evenings.

'Nevaire mind,' he had said in his careful but heavily accented English, 'I will take you sometimes to dance in the evenings. Maman will permit that you go if I chaperone you.'

Ann had laughed. The idea of being chaperoned was novel and enormously old-fashioned when she thought of the freedom she had at home. Mother and Dad never objected to her going out with her friends provided she told them where she was going and provided she was always home at the specified time. Since she had left school at the end of the summer term, her parents had allowed her plenty of liberty, knowing that at eighteen she was sufficiently sensible and mature not to abuse their trust.

Of course, they did know all her friends. The girls were all school chums or the daughters of her parents' friends. The boys—there were about six currently on her writing list—were friends of her nineteen-year-old brother James. She had never been out with anyone as old as Luc Menton. She was looking forward to the widening of her horizons—to being really grown-up at last. At eighteen, she felt neither a girl nor a woman but a bit of both. She could still lapse into helpless giggles with one of her school friends; yet inside she felt the urge to grasp the real meaning of life; to be able to understand what it was all about.

This year in Switzerland was the answer to all her needs. Apart from one or two holidays with her parents—a brief visit to Yugoslavia and another to Majorca, she had never been abroad; never lived abroad. She felt the experience would enormously widen her horizons and help her to decide what exactly she wished to do with her life.

Her parents were not particularly wealthy nor by any means hard up. Father was a dentist and they lived comfortably. But even if they could afford to keep her in idleness at home, Ann's own temperament would not have allowed it. She wanted to be independent, earn her own living, and make something of herself. The problem was what? She had a certain talent for

English; also for drawing and painting but neither was sufficiently strong or marked to give her a vocation. She wished she were more like her friend Marion who had known since she was fourteen that the only thing she wished to be was a nurse.

During this year, Ann decided, she would find out what she wanted to do. It would be a year to grow up in; to sort herself out as a person and decide her future.

Luc Menton, a tall, strongly built, athletic looking young man, brought her out of her daydream by explaining that she must now try on ski-boots which would then be fitted with the skis so that the bindings were safe and would hold her feet in the right position. He seemed to think this important so Ann endeavoured to give the matter her concentration.

Once or twice, she managed to identify a French word or phrase and was delighted with herself. She had passed French O level examination at school and felt she ought to have understood a great deal more but somehow the rapid way everyone spoke, the real French accent, made it seem almost another language to the one she had learned at school.

'It will come very soon to you,' Madame Menton had said the night before when she had shown Ann to her room, Pierre's room, as it happened, which would be hers for the next year. Ann had travelled out alone yesterday, by air to Geneva. But for Luc meeting her at the airport, she felt she would never have arrived safely with all her luggage at Aiguille.

'It was kind of your son to meet me,' she thanked Madame Menton politely as the tall, thin Swiss woman showed her where to put her belongings when she unpacked.

Madame, not unlike Luc, with the same soft brown hair and brown eyes, bustled round the room opening wardrobes and drawers. She smiled at Ann.

'It was Luc's idea. He is of very kind disposition. He is a good boy in every way. He has now completed his studies to become the accountant and has the holiday before he must start work in Geneva in April. It is good he will be home a little while to help you to become accustomed to us and our ways. Luc is an excellent skier and will help you to learn.'

'Oh, I'm sure he won't want to be bothered,' Ann said anxiously. 'It's not right that he should spoil his holiday looking after me!'

'On the contrary,' Madame had told her. 'He is much pleased to have the opportunity to improve his English which is not so good. Italian and German he can speak fluently but English is not so facile for him and he wishes to make this language better. I have told him that it is not good for you always to speak English; that you are here to learn French. So he has agreed that it will be half and half between you.'

So far, Ann thought smiling, it wasn't possible to go 'half and half'. She couldn't follow any French conversation as yet and despite what his mother had said, Luc's English was really very good.

Madame would not permit her to work her first day.

'You will need equipment for ski-ing,' she said, 'and it is better you do this on a weekday. At the weekends, we have many visitors from the valley for the ski-ing and the shop is very full and requires much waiting. Luc will take you down this morning. I have asked him also to show you the places of the shops where you might require to buy certain things, and he will take you also to show you where are the nursery slopes. You will be free two days of the week from work and on these days, Luc will teach you the ski-ing.'

So there it was, all arranged. There was nothing for Ann to worry about, plan, arrange. Madame seemed to have everything organised and all she, Ann, had to do was sit back and enjoy herself.

The morning had begun with a visit to the bank to change some of her travellers cheques. Since Madame was paying her pocket money for her services at the club, she had only to draw enough money for her equipment. Some of this, Luc told her, would be returned to her at the end of her stay for the skis and boots could be re-sold if she so wished before going back to England.

They were now left at the shop for the bindings to be altered. Luc tucked his arm through Ann's and led her up the ice-covered road to the little bar where hot chocolate piled with whipped cream, was served to them.

'It's delicious!' Ann sighed, tasting hers. 'But I mustn't do this every day. I shall get so fat!'

Luc Menton smiled. Ann thought he

looked very attractive when the customary rather serious expression of his face dissolved in humour.

'You are certainly not too fat!' he told her, swinging his long legs in their tight navy ski-pants down from the bar stool. 'Our Swiss girls for the most part are plump. To me, you appear very slim.'

'It's these clothes!' Ann laughed, surveying the tight black ski-pants that were certainly flattering to any figure which didn't boast a big seat! Over them, she wore a thick black and white heavy-knit pullover. Her white anorak, Luc had hung on a hook on the wall behind her. The place was fairly empty. Those who were not at work were ski-ing, Luc informed her.

Ann was suddenly conscious of Luc's admiring gaze and was annoyed to feel her cheeks burning. It seemed as if the Swiss were much more obvious than the English in showing how they felt. Luc's glance was personal and direct. Somehow, she would have found it easier to cope if he had said, like one of the boys at home: 'You've got a smashing figure!' She could have countered that with a smart reply. There was nothing to be said to a look!

But it was not only Luc who was admiring Ann's slim, blonde beauty. Coming towards them was a sun-bronzed dark-haired man with extraordinary brilliant blue eyes, darkly fringed with lashes as long as a girl's.

He spoke rapidly in French to Luc who, Ann surmised from his tone since she could not understand the words, answered rather coolly. However, he made the required introduction. 'May I present Paul Duret—Mademoiselle Elgar.'

Before Ann realised what was happening, the newcomer had taken her hand and was kissing it in the continental fashion. Since it was the first time anyone had ever kissed her hand, Ann was not sure how it should be done, but thinking about it later, it struck her that Paul Duret's lips had stayed overlong against her skin. But she couldn't be sure. It was difficult to be sure of anything because those extraordinary blue eyes seemed to hold her gaze in almost mesmeric fashion. It was Luc's voice which broke the strange moment.

'We must be going, Ann!'

Obediently, she slid down from the bar stool and reached out her arm to take down her anorak. Before she could do so, Paul Duret had possession of it. He stood behind her and as she put her arms into the sleeves, lifted the nylon jacket around her shoulders and with the gentlest of pressures, tucked it around and beneath her chin. Glancing up, Ann saw Luc frowning. It crossed her mind briefly that whoever this man was, he was not a friend of Luc's. Yet Paul Duret was smiling at Luc and patting him on the shoulder.

'I will see you at the club later, *mon cher!*' he said in English and turning to Ann: 'You, also, I hope, Mademoiselle. I look forward to our next meeting.'

There was no mistake this time, Ann thought, as she left the little bar with Luc silent and thoughtful beside her. Paul Duret found her attractive.

The thought gave her a little thrill of excitement. It was somehow more of a compliment when an older man took notice of you. It meant that he saw her as a woman—not as a schoolgirl. She wondered how old he was and on impulse, asked Luc.

'I am not sure!' Luc replied, his voice cold and almost unfriendly. 'Thirty or so. I do not know.'

'Does he live here in Aiguille?' Ann pursued, a little surprised by her own persistence, for she had sensed that Luc did not like the man and perhaps preferred not to talk about him.

'For the season, yes. He has an apartment.'

'The season?'

'Until March. Then he returns to Paris where he lives. He is...an actor, of sorts!'

'That explains his good looks,' Ann answered innocently. 'He really is very handsome, isn't he?'

Luc's face remained impassive as he strode along the road beside her, one hand lightly supporting her arm lest she should slip on the icy surface.

'As I am a man, I do not view Paul Duret as women see him!' he said with the slightest shade of sarcasm. 'I believe, however, he is considered very attractive to women.'

Ann let the subject of Paul Duret drop. After all, she was not really interested—only curious. In an indefinable way, Luc's unspoken objection to Paul had stimulated that curiosity. Luc had struck her as very easy going, a gregarious, friendly young man. She wished she could ask him outright *why* he disliked the older man who had greeted him so warmly. But Luc was almost as much a stranger to her as Paul Duret himself and it was none of her business, anyway.

'Curiosity killed the cat!' her brother, James, was always telling her. But she couldn't help this unfortunate trait in her character. People fascinated her; what motivated them; what they thought; why they behaved as they did; what attracted people to one another.

'It's none of your business, Ann!' James said over and over again.

Dear James! Ann thought with a sudden stab of homesickness. She adored her only brother. He was close enough to her in age for them to have become wonderful friends since their teens, though earlier they had quarrelled like cat and dog! Now, they went everywhere together, shared friends and parties and the process of growing up. She wondered how James was getting along with Pierre. If Pierre was as nice as his brother, Luc, then she was certain James was enjoying his company. She eagerly awaited her brother's first letter to her, telling her about the Swiss boy's arrival and the family's reactions. This afternoon, if Madame Menton did not require her help she would write her own first letter home, she decided.

The sun, now that it was nearly mid-day, was high above them in the postcard blue sky. It was very hot—almost too hot for Ann to wish to be wearing her anorak as well as the thick ski-jumper beneath.

'Isn't it marvellous!' she said to Luc. 'February and as hot as this! What will it be like in March?'

Luc smiled. Once again Ann thought how attractive he looked when he did so. He should smile more often. He was obviously a very serious young man. Used as she was to James' rather frivolous attitude to life, Luc was an odd contrast. But then, the three years between nineteen and twenty-two did change a boy into a man. By the time James was twenty-two, no doubt he would have sobered up a little and ceased to take life as one big joke. Her father was always telling him it was high time he began to think seriously of his future. Luc had long since done so.

'Were your examinations difficult?' she asked Luc. 'Your mother told me you had passed your finals successfully.'

Luc glanced down at the girl beside him

and then conscious that he was staring, quickly looked away. He felt a totally unaccustomed shyness with her which he could not explain. He considered himself past the age when girls confused and embarrassed him! Yet this English girl did both. He was finding it hard to follow her quick changes of thought; the directness of her questions; the almost childlike way in which she demanded explanations and answers from him. She had a way of looking directly into his eyes—not challenging yet totally trusting.

'Yes!' he told himself, 'at her age one can be totally trusting.' At his, one knew better. How incredibly naïve he had been at eighteen. When Ingeborg Tissier had smiled at him for the first time, he had trustingly laid his heart at her feet. That she would one day trample upon it as so much dust had never then crossed his mind.

How deeply and totally and sincerely he had loved the tall Swiss-German girl with her magnificent Junoesque figure and quick, clever intellect and wit! How completely he had fallen under the spell of her throaty contralto voice singing German lieder and Swiss folk songs as they skied together over the mountains and walked hand in hand through the pine forests in summer with a crowd of other teenagers, Ingeborg's friends and admirers.

It was easy enough now to see the real picture—Ingeborg the Queen and all the rest of them her courtiers to whom she doled out her favours. He wasn't the only boy madly in love with her. All the others were, too, and she had known it and used them, playing one against the other through that long tormented year.

'Do not be jealous, my little Luc!' How tender and hypnotic her deep voice. 'I only pretend to care for the others. It is you I love.'

He had trusted, believed...right up to the very last day when he had discovered that all four boys in the group were also her lovers. Outraged, humiliated, filled with self-loathing, he had challenged her to deny what he had been told. She had laughed.

'My poor deluded little boy. Don't pretend you didn't *know*.'

But he had not known. Perhaps because he hadn't wanted to know. She was the sun round which he had orbited along with all her other satellites, believing he was the only one.

Even now, four years later, the bitter taste still lay in his mouth, clouding his relationships with other girls he had subsequently met. He would look at them, and wonder...are they, too, like Inge? He took them to dances, kissed them, found himself falling a little in love with them and quickly drew back from the encounter. He had acquired the nickname among his contemporaries of Papillon—a butterfly who flitted from girl to girl with apparent indifference. It was a name he did not care for, knowing that it belied the real depth and seriousness of his nature. He flitted only because he could no longer believe; no longer trust. Such was the damage Inge had done him.

He had not been exactly pleased when his mother and father had told him of the exchange arrangements that had been made between them and the English family, Elgar. He realised that the year in England would be enormously beneficial to Pierre but he did not like the idea of the English girl coming to live with them as one of the family. He had made the acquaintance of several English girls who came out to ski at Aiguille. It was essentially an exclusive little resort with three very chic hotels for the rich and the women who came were wives or daughters of well-to-do men. He, himself, was of good middle-class stock and his parents were far from poor. The club was making a great deal of money and had done better and better as the years went by and Aiguille increased in popularity as a select winter sports resort. But he did not care for the ultra-rich: their high-pitched artificial voices; their assumption that the world was at their feet and the rest of the people there to serve them. They monopolised the ski-lifts, the sun terraces, the bars and the dance floors as if it were all their right, whereas their money entitled them only to the use of the place, not their ownership.

He found his feelings hard to define exactly. The winter and summer visitors did not make him feel inferior but in some odd way, superior; as if *they* were the butterflies flitting from pleasure to pleasure without thought of others or of anything but their own enjoyment. Life, he felt, should be taken more seriously.

'Do not be silly, Luc!' his mother had once chided him when he had tried to voice his views. 'These people are on holiday. It is natural they should seek pleasure. Would you have them be serious when perhaps it is only for these few weeks in the year they may forget their responsibilities and be thoughtless and gay? You have done too much studying. It is time you were a little thoughtless and gay yourself!'

But Luc did not feel carefree. He knew there was something wrong but could not name it. His work had gone well. He had qualified in his chosen career and he had nothing to worry about.

'All the same, Maman,' he had told her the day before Ann Elgar's arrival, 'I do not look forward with pleasure to having the English girl live with us. It is bound to spoil our family unity. We will be forced to be always on our best behaviour; to watch what we say and how we say it!'

'It will not be that way at all,' his mother had argued. 'This girl is not coming to change us but to become one of us. It is she who must make the adaptation. We will be as we always are and she must fit in with us.'

'Oh, well!' Luc had terminated the conversation. 'It will be good for my

English and in any event, it is only until April. I dare say I shall survive!'

Perhaps because he felt a little conscience-stricken about his unwillingness to have the girl, Luc finally behaved with customary reversal of his true feelings. He put himself out to make the four-hour journey to Geneva and met Ann at the airport—simply because it was the very last thing he wished to do.

His first glimpse of her had confused him with his pre-conceived ideas about English girls. She looked very much younger than he anticipated—almost boyish with that short, cropped fair hair and elfin-shaped oval face. She was standing by the Customs counter looking like a small, lost schoolgirl, not knowing what to do next.

Later, in the train, she chatted to him easily and quite unself-consciously about herself.

'I'm awfully glad you came to meet me,' she had thanked him warmly. 'I expect you think I'm an awful fool but I've never travelled outside England by myself. I kept thinking what would happen if I got the wrong train and arrived at the wrong place. With my limited French, I knew I'd never understand directions and platforms and so on. I suppose it's my own fault, really. At home, I always leave all that kind of thing to James, my brother.'

Somehow, the journey back to Aiguille had passed in what seemed a few minutes. Ann told him about her home, her parents, her school, her brother. She described the house and the room his brother Pierre would sleep in.

She had laughed then, at her own thoughts.

'Just think!' she told him. 'Your brother and I must have passed each other in the air and I'll be living in his room and he in mine and yet we've never met. Tell me about him. Do you think he and James will hit it off?'

Luc smiled now at the memory. Ann had disarmed him despite his intended indifference—even dislike of her. It was the child-like quality that entranced him. She was fresh and unspoilt, natural and uninhibited. Yet for all her naïvety, she was not gauche. Her physical movements were neat and graceful; she was composed and yet bubbling over with excitement and pleasure which was infectious. He'd known then that his mother would be enchanted by her; his father, too.

Perhaps I, also! Luc told himself as he guided her down the street. For a moment his face relaxed in a smile but almost at once, it stiffened again. He was not the only one to find young Ann Elgar attractive. Paul Duret had not even bothered to try to disguise his sentiments.

And that is one thing I will not permit! Luc thought, his own intense dislike for the French actor sending a swift course of anger through him. But gradually it simmered down as he told himself logically: 'He may be attracted to her, but she will not be interested in him. To a girl of eighteen, a man of thirty would seem very old.

He could not know that while he walked in silence with his thoughts, Ann, too, was lost in thought—thoughts of the strange, mesmeric eyes of the sun-tanned man called Paul.

2

The mid-day meal was eaten by the family in the club. It seemed to Ann to be an enormous repast, beginning with a thick vegetable soup, followed by spaghetti bolognaise and finally veal in a delicious sauce with vegetables, and to complete the meal, a large cup of coffee.

'I shall soon become very fat!' she said to Madame Menton in her best French. Madame nodded.

'And very good, too. You are far too thin, is she not, Luc?'

Luc gave Ann a friendly smile.

'I think she is just right!' he said amicably.

Ann relaxed happily in her chair. Luc was obviously going to be a real friend—a kind of benign elder brother. In a way, she would appreciate him more than James who was forever teasing her. No compliments ever from him—the very reverse. Not that she minded. She was well used to being ragged. Even her boyfriends teased her and she never objected. She had acquired various nicknames from James and his friends—Shrimp, Button-nose because hers was retroussé, Fourpence—a silly name really because she had a childish habit of stamping her foot when she was trying to make a point in an argument. She was glad suddenly to have left all those relics of childhood behind her. Here, no one knew her silly nicknames and she was treated as a young woman of her age should be treated.

Monsieur Menton, Luc's father, was a round, jovial little man; as jolly and extroverted as Luc was quiet and thoughtful. He spoke practically no English and Ann was forced to converse with him in her schoolroom French which sent his rather red face into big crinkly smiles.

The club itself was unlike anything Ann had ever seen at home. It was a rambling wooden chalet type building with a huge sun veranda to one side and a skating rink on the other. It seemed to her as if everyone in Aiguille must be congregated here for there was not a table or chair free; the sun terrace was crowded with skiers and there were dozens more crowding round the small bar. The waiters were rushed off their feet serving 'curlings'—a brandy-based long drink the skiers seemed particularly to enjoy; coffee, hot chocolate with layers of whippped cream on top, *oranges pressés*—which were literally the juice of freshly squeezed oranges; and, or course, meals. The air was filled with smoke, noise and talk and their own little corner table, reserved for the Patron's family, was an oasis in the general confusion.

'You see how it is here!' Madame Menton said, noting Ann's glances round the room. 'I have never enough help at the peak times. By one o'clock, the room will be nearly empty and except for a few more elderly people who cannot ski sunning themselves on the terraces, the club will remain empty until about half past three when the skiers begin to return. We are then frantically busy once more throughout the tea-dance until six. After that it is quiet until the evening dance at nine-thirty, but you will not be required to help then.'

Ann had already learned from her mother through letters exchanged between her and Madame Menton, what her duties would be; helping to serve coffees and drinks to the customers.

'Glorified waitress!' James had said grinning. But Ann didn't in the least mind doing such a job. 'Why should I?' she returned tartly. 'We often had to wait on table at school *and* do the washing up on Sundays!'

Now she felt even happier about the job although just a shade nervous that she might not understand the demands of the customers. This evening she would ask Luc to run through all the names of all the drink and food people might ask her for in French. She had a good enough memory. It shouldn't be too difficult and she was determined to make a success of the job. Madame Menton was paying her the equivalent of five pounds a week in Swiss francs for pocket money and she intended to earn it. She had personally thought it very unlikely that she would need so much spending money. This morning in the sports shop, Luc had disillusioned her.

'You will find it quite costly paying for the ski lifts,' he told her. 'It is best to buy a big book of tickets. I will get one for you and you can repay me when you have been to the bank.'

After lunch Luc took her for her first ski-ing lesson. He carried her skis with his own to the flattest of the nursery slopes and showed her how to fasten them. Ann was shocked to find that far from being able to ski, she could not even stand up properly. With every movement of her body, she felt the skis sliding away beneath her and Luc had to steady her by the arm.

'I'll never manage!' she gasped after five minutes just attempting to stay upright.

Luc laughed.

'Oh, yes, you will. You must persevere, Ann. It will suddenly come to you. Try now to come a little downhill. It is sometimes easier to balance when you are moving.'

She fell at least fifteen times in as many minutes. Each time Luc helped her to her feet and encouraged her to try again.

'I can't!' Ann gasped. 'I'm aching all over and I'll never do it.'

'Look!' Luc replied, pointing to a toddler of about four years old who went speeding down the slope in front of them. 'If that infant can manage it, so can you!'

For a further half hour Ann struggled to keep her balance. At last, she managed to travel about twenty yards without falling and she turned to Luc triumphantly, her cheeks glowing.

'I did it! I actually did it!' she cried.

Luc was laughing outright.

'You're not to laugh at me!' Ann said, with mock indignation. 'I'm proud of myself!'

'And I am proud of you,' Luc said, though his eyes were still full of laughter. 'Come, I will show you what it feels like really to ski. We will go down there together. I will support you from behind.'

Ann looked down the slope and gasped.

'I couldn't go down there!' she said aghast. 'I'd fall every yard of the way!'

'No, you won't,' Luc said confidently. 'I will stand behind you, my skis outside yours and support you. It is not a very big slope when all is said and done. If we fall we shall not damage ourselves much. Trust me, Ann. It will give you pleasure, I'm sure.'

Ann sighed.

'You're daring me, aren't you, Luc? I never could resist a dare. All right, I'll go wherever and however you suggest.'

Luc made her stand still while he manoeuvred himself into the best position behind her. He stuck his batons in the snow and clasped her round the waist.

'Now relax!' he cautioned her. 'Bend

36

your knees as I have been showing you and leave everything else to me.'

There was a moment or two when he pushed off when Ann was sure this was a mistake and that it would end in disaster. But suddenly, they were sliding down the slope, their speed increasing steadily and she knew for the first time what a bird must feel like flying. All fear was gone. Luc's arms were tightly round her waist and she gave herself up to the joy of movement. The wind rushed past her cheeks, icy cold and yet exhilarating.

'I'm ski-ing—really ski-ing!' she thought and could have shouted aloud with sheer joy. But they were now at the bottom of the slope and in his attempt to halt them, Luc's skis touched hers and the next moment they were in a tangled heap in the snow. Ann's mouth, hair and eyes were full of it.

'Are you all right, Ann? You are not hurt?'

The anxiety in Luc's voice brought Ann back to reality. She wiped the snow from her face and looked up at him laughing.

'I'm fine and it was absolutely *marvellous!*' she cried.

He stood up and began to straighten her

skis, his face relaxed once more and happy as he surveyed her flushed, contented face.

'I really skied!' she said, childishly boasting. 'I really did, didn't I?'

He hadn't the heart to tell her that they had just traversed the very easiest of beginner's slopes—so easy that even the tiniest toddlers attacked it without fear. This was not the moment to let her know how much she had to learn before she could claim to be a skier! She hadn't even managed it alone. But it was more than enough for him to realise her pleasure and excitement in the sport he loved so much. Now he had whetted her appetite for it, there would be no holding her. She was slim, athletic, naturally graceful. One day she would make a good skier and he would take her up on the Point d'Aiguille—the mountain known as the Needle Point from which the village derived its name.

As he helped her upright, her face was very close to his. Her eyes were very bright, very blue as they looked into his.

'Oh, Luc!' she said again, her voice breathless and husky with excitement. 'It was wonderful fun!'

That was the moment, quite recognisable, instantaneous and never-to-be forgotten, when he fell in love with her. He looked back wordlessly into her eyes and no longer took in the meaning of her words. He was aware only of how much he wanted to kiss those softly parted lips.

Suddenly her face clouded, her voice filled with regret.

'I am a selfish pig!' she said. 'Just because it has all been so exciting for me, I took it for granted it must be for you, too. You've wasted a whole afternoon trying to keep me upright when you could have been really ski-ing.'

Words returned to him as he quickly reassured her.

'I can do what you call proper ski-ing any time,' he told her. 'It is not every day I have the opportunity to help a beginner to make their first steps. One day when you are an Olympic champion, I shall be able to boast that it was I who began the ball to roll, no?'

Ann giggled happily. Quite unselfconsciously, she tucked her arm through Luc's for support as they worked their way on their skis towards the lift. She looked at it with dismay.

'How on earth do you go up on a thing like that?' she asked, staring at the overhead cable with the long steel poles dangling from it at intervals of about twelve feet. 'I shall fall off, I'm sure!'

But it was surprisingly easy to tuck the plastic disk between her skis and lean her seat back against it for support. As the pole took her weight, there was a moment of anxiety when she nearly wobbled to one side but soon she was balanced and enjoying the short ride to the top. Half way up she realised that she had forgotten to ask Luc how to become detached from the contraption. Anxiously she watched the two people ahead of her, saw them lift the pole away from them and push it off as they turned right and halted on the flat snow to one side.

A moment or two later she was attempting the same thing and found herself once more flat on her back. Luc, arriving behind her, helped her up and she leaned against him gasping.

'I'm exhausted!' she admitted. 'I don't think I could go another step.'

Luc bent down and detached her skis. Now her feet and legs and ankles were all throbbing.

'Wait here whilst I collect our batons,' Luc told her. Gratefully, she stood still, watching the skiers, feeling cool air brush against her cheeks where the sun had already begun to tan them. She felt tired, aching, but blissfully happy. No wonder everyone was always laughing, happy, gay. It must be quite impossible to feel depressed in a place like this.

'I would offer you a drink, Ann, but I think it is best we go straight home so that you can take a hot bath,' Luc said as they walked away from the ski lift towards the road, Luc carrying both pairs of skis as if they were no weight at all. 'You will be very stiff, I expect. I will ask Maman to give you one of the pine tablets for your bath. You will find them very refreshing.'

Lying in the funny half-sized bath, the green, hot water steaming aromatically round her, Ann breathed in the scent of pine and realised just how right Luc had been. It was wonderfully refreshing, especially as she was beginning really to stiffen up. Luc had explained that ski-ing used many muscles one did not use in ordinary everyday life. Just about all of them, judging by the way I feel, Ann thought, as she let the water relax her limbs.

She changed into slacks and a shirt which Madame had written to say was quite acceptable après ski wear. The slacks were pale blue, flared a little at the ankle and very becoming; the jumper, bought at Marks and Sparks, matched perfectly. Last night, Ann had not changed out of her travelling suit at Madame's suggestion for she had been tired from the journey and ready for bed immediately after the evening meal. Now, standing in the warm bedroom with its yellow polished wooden floor and gay curtains and rugs, she surveyed her reflection in the mirror with cheerful pleasure. Pale blue suited her and with the light tan she had acquired already, she looked well and at her best.

In one corner of the room Pierre's desk of carved wood was covered with photographs—mostly taken of himself and Luc ski-ing. Ann looked at them closely for the first time. She felt a moment of deep regret for poor Pierre missing all the fun. Then common sense told her that this life was every-day to him and that a visit to England no doubt held much more promise of novelty for him. The boy was more like his father than his mother—chubby, with a broad friendly grin. It was hard to think of him and Luc as brothers. Beside him, Luc looked taller even than his six foot; very fair, his eyes serious as he stared into the camera, his skis pointing away, his head turned over his shoulder as if the person taking the picture had just called him at the start of a run. He was poised on his skis, leaning a little on his batons as if about to push himself off.

Memories of the afternoon came back with all the thrill of that last run down. How kind Luc was! She would try to be especially nice to him this evening. And she must help Madame Menton, too. Perhaps she would be allowed to help tonight with the washing up for it seemed as if her hostess had no other help in the home.

When she went downstairs, Luc was also bathed and changed into slacks and a white polo-necked sweater. He was sitting in the salon with his father. As upstairs, the floor and furniture in the salon were of polished wood, shining, spotless and sweet-smelling. The curtains and covers were bright and reminded Ann of the little wooden Swiss chalets sold as musical boxes at home. She *must* find time this evening to write home. There was so much to describe, to tell them. Madame had insisted a telegram was despatched last night announcing her safe arrival but her family could know nothing as yet of the enormous pleasure she was already deriving from her new 'home'.

It had been her intention to assist Madame Menton in the kitchen where she was preparing supper, but Monsieur Menton motioned her into a chair, saying firmly:

'My wife has said you shall not work today, Mademoiselle Ann, so you are to be obedient to her wishes as we all are, eh, Luc?' he ended with a wink and a chuckle.

Luc translated his father's French into English and added:

'Father is quite right. We all do as Maman says in this house!'

But Ann knew very well neither father nor son was in the least scared of Madame. Who could possibly be? For she was kindness and good nature itself.

Luc is just like her! Ann thought as she tried to concentrate on Monsieur Menton's rapid French.

Throughout supper Ann found herself

answering questions about her home. For her own sake, Madame insisted that meal times should be conducted in French. Her efforts made them laugh but their laughter was always kindly. Only Luc did not laugh, correcting her gently and supplying her with the word she wanted. He, himself, had little to say.

'Are you always so quiet?' she asked him when coffee was served in large steaming cups. 'Is he, Madame, or is it that I talk too much? At home I am always being told that I monopolise the conversation. You must tell me to be quiet!'

Madame gave Luc a quick searching look, as if for a moment Ann's words had made her anxious about her son.

'Are you tired, *chéri?*' she asked.

Luc shook his head.

'On the contrary, Maman. I was thinking of inviting Ann to the club to dance—that is, if *you* are not too tired, Ann?'

'Of course she is!' Madame replied at the same moment as Ann said: 'Oh, I'd just love to do that, Luc!'

They all laughed and Madame said:

'Well, for a little while then. But do not keep her out too late, Luc. You understand?'

He nodded.

It was on the tip of Ann's tongue to say that she was often out at dances till one in the morning at home, but she bit back the words just in time. No doubt Madame was remembering that tomorrow she started work and must be fresh. It was only fair that she should be at her best.

'Should I change my clothes?' she asked Luc, but he shook his head.

'You can wear what you wish at the club. Some women wear dresses, some short and even long. Since last year many wear trouser suits and I have even seen culottes which I personally do not fancy. You are quite suitably attired, Ann.'

It was only a short walk across to the club from the Menton's chalet. But now the sun had long since set and the village street was lit with lamps which glittered on the icicles hanging from all the eaves. The snow glittered and was crisp beneath their feet. Summer seemed suddenly to have turned back to winter and Ann gasped as the icy cold air first hit her lungs.

Luc laughed.

'I told you you would need that thick coat,' he said, tucking her ungloved hand into his pocket. 'At night here in this

46

time of year, it freezes. First thing in the morning, the ski slopes will be hard and icy and it is best you do not go on them until the sun thaws the snow a little. Then falling is more comfortable.'

'Oh, I'm having so much fun!' Ann said happily. 'I suppose by now I ought to be feeling a little homesick; wishing myself back with Mum and Dad and James—but I don't. I never want to leave here, Luc. It's all so *lovely!*'

Luc caught his breath. Her simple, childlike enthusiasm was infectious. He had lived in or near this village all his life and had long long ago ceased to see it as Ann now did. He thought of it simply as home, a place to go to at weekends and in his holidays, where there was excellent ski-ing and his mother's good cooking always awaiting him. There had been a time when he was much younger when he had thought of the season as an excellent time for picking up girls, enjoying brief holiday flirtations, dancing with and kissing unattached girls who frequented the club and the night-clubs after dark. But now such brief friendships or romances had lost their novelty and struck him as pointless. At the end of their visit, the girls went back to their homes—Paris, Italy, other towns in Switzerland and he knew he would never see them again, nor even wished to do so. The club really bored him now from long association and but for his love of dancing, he doubted he would go there at night at all.

But now he caught Ann's excitement and it began to infect him. She made everything so different—just by her sheer uncomplicated enthusiasm. Was she always like this? he wondered. It was like being with a bottle of champagne—she bubbled with life and fun. Yet there was nothing of the coquette in her. He had seen no looks such as he was well used to from girls, from beneath half-closed lids; no challenge behind her smile; no expression in her eyes that could be called an invitation. What did she really think of him? He wished very much he knew her well enough to ask.

Luc was well accustomed to the admiring glances and advances of the opposite sex. Tall, bronzed, a first-class skier, it was natural that women stared at him and those who were on the look-out for romance, seldom hid their interest. He did not consider himself to be attractive and yet realised that many women found him so. Perhaps if it had not been for his disastrous experiences with Ingeborg in his adolescent years, he might have taken these women more seriously. As it was, he looked at them with something akin to contempt; certainly mistrustfully. He was not to know that it was this very unresponsiveness that heightened his appeal to them, unconsciously challenging them to try harder to evoke his interest.

Ann was different. She was as natural with him as if he, not the English boy, James, were her brother. Perhaps it was because of her closeness to her brother that she found it easy to be guileless with the opposite sex. He, himself, having no sisters, was much more aware of her as a female than she was of him as a male.

As Luc took Ann into the club and showed her where to hang her coat, he knew that this was not the true explanation. Ann might well see him as a brother but he would never be able to see her as a sister. To him, she was simply the strange adorable little English au pair girl with whom he had quite astonishingly fallen in love.

3

The single large L-shaped room was even more crowded than it had been at lunch time. The bar was filled with smoke and the four-piece band with two amplifiers was almost an assault upon Ann's unprepared eardrums. The tables round the dance floor were all occupied and the floor itself was a seething mass of couples reminiscent of the teenage parties Ann went to at home.

Luc's hand held firmly to her forearm as if he were afraid he would lose her in the crowd.Within minutes, a waiter had produced a table for them not far from the bar and not too near the floor. As they seated themselves, Luc grinned and said:

'If you don't book, you haven't a hope of a table after ten o'clock. It is fortunate for me I am the son of the Patron—otherwise we should not be sitting.'

He ordered a bottle of wine for himself and an *orange pressé* for Ann and then gave up the attempt to make himself heard above the noise of the dance group. Ann watched the dancers with a little tremor of excitement. There were quite a few teenagers here but practically every other age group was represented, too, and she felt in the dim, candle-lit atmosphere the thrill of attending her very first night-club in grown-up sophisticated company. How James would envy her if he could see her now!

Luc, watching the absorbed expression on her face, tried to see the familiar scene through her eyes. A little of her excitement transferred to him and he covered her hand where it lay on the tablecloth and said:

'You like it here?'

'Oh, yes!' Ann replied without hesitation, her eyes large and sparkling. 'I've never been anywhere like this at home. It's a wonderful group, too. Who are they, Luc?'

'It is an English group,' Luc explained. 'They call themselves The Four Saints. Wait until you hear them play their signature tune, *The Saints Go Marching In*. They really are outstanding and everyone stops talking, drinking, dancing, to listen.

The waiter arrived with their drinks and Ann sipped the iced orange juice in happy contentment.

'You like dancing?' Luc asked when the noise quietened for a softer French tune with a haunting melody Ann did not recognise.

'Oh, yes!' she replied. 'But I've never danced to anything but pop. I can't waltz or tango or anything—at least, not very well. We had compulsory ballroom dancing lessons at my school but everybody loathed them. I suppose I *could*, if I tried.'

'Like ski-ing!' Luc smiled back. 'I will have to teach you because only about one in three dances played here are pop. I, too, enjoy this, but the other kind of dancing is nice, too. You will not find it difficult, I am sure, especially when the floor is so crowded. It is difficult to move.'

Ann looked once more at the couples dancing now in a tight embrace. There was even one couple kissing.

'I see what you mean!' she said impishly to Luc. 'At least no one can see your feet if you put a foot wrong!'

'Mademoiselle, may I have the pleasure?'

Ann looked up and felt her whole face suffuse with colour as she met the strange, burning glance of Paul Duret. He was bowing towards her, inviting her to dance. She looked quickly at Luc and noticed that his eyebrows were drawn together in a frown he wasn't even troubling to conceal. Before she could reply, he said coldly:

'I'm afraid Mademoiselle Elgar has just agreed to have this dance with me.'

The man did not even look at Luc. He merely smiled at Ann and said easily:

'Then with your permission, Mademoiselle, I will return a little later?'

She nodded and Paul Duret moved away from their table and elbowed his way back to the bar. There he lent on one arm, his back towards the bar, staring at her. Quickly she looked away and back to Luc.

'Well, ought we not to dance?' she asked confused. 'I mean, you said we were going to. It looks so rude if...'

'I do not care if Duret thinks me rude. You may as well know, Ann, that I do not like the man and certainly do not count him among my friends. I prefer that he does not dance with you and I hope that I made this quite clear to him.'

Ann felt an unexpected stab of annoyance.

'But why not?' she asked. 'What's wrong with him? What on earth is wrong with dancing with him? I don't see why you

54

should try to stop me if *I* wish it.'

'Do you?' Luc asked, looking at her in such a penetrating and direct manner that her confusion mounted.

'Well, I don't see why not!' she prevaricated. 'You haven't given me a reason why not, Luc. What is wrong with him?'

'He is too old for you!' Luc said after a moment's hesitation. His words released Ann from the peculiar tension that had held her since Paul Duret had invited her to dance. She laughed.

'Oh, Luc, you are silly!' she said. 'I'm not a child. I'm quite old enough to choose my own friends. As to dancing with him—well, I can't see what harm that could do anyone.'

Yet even as she spoke, she had a sudden swift picture of herself held in Paul Duret's arms as she had seen those other couples, tightly clasped in an embrace that seemed to have very little to do with dancing. The colour came back into her cheeks and she dropped her eyes from Luc's, suddenly self-conscious again and ill at ease with him.

She heard his voice, cold and unfriendly: 'You must, of course, do as you wish.'

Ann's happiness seemed to have evaporated without warning. She couldn't understand Luc's behaviour. Even if he did not personally like Paul Duret, what harm was there in her having one dance with him? All this embarrassment would have been avoided if Luc hadn't made a fuss.

'Well, don't let's quarrel about it!' she said simply. 'It isn't important. Can't we dance, Luc? I'd love to if you would.'

With a conscious effort Luc fought off his ill humour. He was, after all, making a mountain out of a molehill. Ann had given no indication of being interested in Duret so he was jumping the gun trying to protect her from the Frenchman. Moreover, he was making himself appear boorish in her eyes.

He stood up at once and guided her onto the crowded floor. To Ann's relief, they were playing an old Beatles tune and she thoroughly enjoyed the easy, uninhibited movements familiar to her from parties at home. Luc seemed to have cheered up and was dancing opposite her effortlessly and gracefully. She felt happy again and full of the sheer joy of living. It was all so much fun.

Although there was little chance on so

crowded a floor to move very far, they were gradually circling the room and half way through the dance Ann, flinging back her head, found herself looking directly past Luc's face into the unsmiling eyes of Paul Duret. He was barely six feet away from her, standing by the end of the bar watching her.

The instant of confusion gave way to a sudden daredevil rush of excitement. Instead of her dancing becoming more restrained beneath those staring, watchful eyes, it became less so.

'I am terrible!' she thought with an inward giggle. 'I'm behaving very badly. I'm dancing with Luc and flirting with Paul Duret and Luc doesn't know and I ought not to be doing this!'

But she didn't care. She was having so much fun. She felt keyed up, excited and yet quite at ease. Her awareness of the older man watching her was acting like a jet of adrenalin in her veins.

Sometime later the dance ended and Luc took her off the floor back to their table. She was flushed, breathless and laughing. She knew, without looking at Paul Duret, that he was still watching her.

Luc had enjoyed the dance, too. He was smiling again and congratulating her on her performance.

'I was very proud to be with you,' he said gallantly. 'A lot of people were observing you!'

For a moment Ann was afraid he had noticed Paul but he went on cheerfully:

'You are a very good dancer. I think it will be easy to teach you other kinds of dancing. You have much rhythm.'

The group were taking a rest. The room was comparatively quiet by the dance floor and the noise had shifted to the opposite end where a number of guests, mostly men, were disappearing behind a green baize curtain.

'What are they doing?' Ann asked curiously. 'Is there another bar there?'

'No, it is the Boule,' Luc said. And seeing her mystified expression, explained the simple little gambling game that was attracting the visitors. As far as she could make out, it was not unlike roulette.

A quick glance round the room told her that Paul Duret must also have gone through to gamble. He was no longer at the bar. But she had no doubt in her mind he would come back; that he would ask her to dance and that this time she would give Luc no chance to answer for her. She would say 'yes'!

Luc appeared to have forgotten about Paul. He was talking once more in his easy, friendly way, pointing out various people he knew and introducing her to two of the ski instructors who came over to greet him. A young woman also approached them whom he introduced as Mademoiselle Marie Jouer. She was a tall, dark, attractive girl with an Italian-type face and colouring, of about Luc's age. Later, he told her that Marie was the daughter of one of the local hotel owners and had been a school mate and friend of the Menton family since they were all babies.

'She is very beautiful!' Ann said enviously. 'I always wanted to be tall and dark and mysterious—a sort of Mona Lisa type like Marie!'

Luc looked surprised.

'Marie—beautiful? Well, I suppose she is attractive. To me she's just Marie—a wonderful skier and an excellent linguist. She is receptionist now for her father at L'Hotel d'Alpine—a very nice girl indeed. I'm very fond of her.'

He spoke warmly and yet Ann sensed

that Marie was nothing very special in Luc's life—at least, not from his point of view. She was not quite so sure Marie was as immune to Luc's charms as he was to hers. Although Marie's conversation seemed easy and casual, the look she had given Ann was penetrating and questioning, as if she might be personally concerned about Luc's private life.

The thought crossed Ann's mind that Marie had no cause to be jealous of her. Luc was just being kind to her, showing her the ropes, as he might well do for any other guest in his house.

'Mademoiselle?'

Once again, Paul Duret's voice brought her out of her private daydream. She had not been aware that the music had started up again, or that Paul Duret had approached their table.

She glanced swiftly at Luc but his face was impassive and he made no move to prevent her accepting the invitation. She stood up and felt Paul Duret's hand touch her elbow lightly as he guided her onto the floor. The next moment she was in his arms.

To Ann's surprise and chagrin, she found herself trembling with what she took to be nerves. The tune was an Italian one, soft, romantic and dreamy. She was not sure what kind of dance was entailed, and felt certain she would stumble and make a fool of herself. But she need not have worried. The slight pressure of her partner's body along the length of her own, guided her skilfully into the rhythm so that in a moment she was able to forget her feet and let her attention wander.

The face of the man, so close to hers, was deeply tanned as if he spent a great deal of time in the sun. There were little lines around his eyes and mouth which made him look suddenly older than she had supposed, yet at the same time, attracted her. She remembered that Luc had placed Paul's age at around thirty. He couldn't possibly have any real interest in a girl of eighteen. She decided that he, like Luc, was just being nice to her. When he discovered how empty and meaningless her life had been, how devoid of experience in anything beyond school, he would soon become bored with her and her conversation. She would probably not be asked for a second dance, she told herself.

But at that moment Paul Duret pulled her just a shade closer to him and his cheek seemed to lay quite naturally against hers. She was nervous and yet at the same time, oddly excited by his proximity. She did not understand her reactions.

It was by no means the first time she had danced cheek to cheek with her partner; smooch dancing was common practice at all the dances she had been to at home and usually, if anyone turned out the lights, some fairly passionate kissing went on during the dancing. But this was different in a subtle way she could not understand. Was it, she asked herself, because Paul Duret was a man—not a boy? Because she felt out of her depth with him? He was very attractive. When he drew his face away from hers for a moment to look down into her eyes, she found herself powerless to look away.

'You are trembling,' he said softly, his English accent even more heavily pronounced than Luc's. 'You are not cold?'

'Oh, no!' Ann replied instantly. The room was stifling. She felt the colour come back into her cheeks and was suddenly furious with herself for behaving so childishly. 'I'm just a little nervous,' she admitted in a rush of words that wouldn't be held back. 'You see, I've never been to a real night-club before and this kind of dancing is new to me, too, so I'm worried in case I do anything stupid.'

As she listened to herself talking, she wished herself safely back at the table with Luc. It was too ridiculous. With her one ambition to appear grown-up and worldly-wise, she had opened her mouth and virtually voiced her lack of sophistication.

But her companion did not seem in the least put out. He was smiling in the kindest possible way and saying:

'You must not be nervous of anything when you are with me, Mademoiselle!'

'Oh, don't call me that. Call me Ann,' she replied still not at ease with him.

'I would be enchanted!' he answered with the slightest pressure of his hand on hers. 'And you must call me Paul.' He pronounced his name 'Powell' in the French manner but she used the English intonation and he was once more smiling at her.

'It sounds a little strange but very charming,' he said. 'Now tell me how are you enjoying your stay at Aiguille?'

Suddenly Ann felt herself relax. She was no longer in awe of him. He had a way of putting her at her ease, listening to her chatter as if it really interested him; nodding as she spoke as if her words were really profound. She found herself laughing with her natural gaiety.

'It's all so new and such fun!' she said. 'I know I'm going to love every minute of it.'

'And we in Aiguille are going to love having anyone so young and beautiful, and so full of life,' Paul replied.

His compliments, given in a low, intense voice, made her self-conscious again. She was not sorry when he withdrew that strange hypnotic glance and laid his cheek once more to hers.

They danced for several minutes in silence. Ann became intensely aware of his body laid against her own. He was not as tall as Luc and much more solidly built but strong and very muscular. She realised that she was becoming sexually very conscious of him and told herself not to be so ridiculous. She had nothing against sex and she always enjoyed kissing and being kissed, provided she liked the boy embracing her. But she believed firmly in keeping control of any situation in which her physical emotions were involved. She and her girl friends had discussed the subject endlessly at school and were all agreed that it was a good idea to have lots of boy friends and lots of experience provided it stayed within reasonable limits. Not for them the promiscuous love affairs talked about on T.V and written about warningly in magazines and stories. They all intended to keep the real love-making for the boy they really loved, and as far as Ann was concerned, she knew she had never been in love yet. There had been several romances when she'd imagined she was in love but all the time, deep down inside, she'd known it wasn't the Real Thing. She'd known she'd just wanted a big romance and built up her own romantic thoughts around a boy she had particularly liked. There had even been moments when she felt sufficiently sexually aroused to know that one part of her wanted a great deal more than a few kisses and embraces; that the boy had wanted more, too. But she had always drawn back from such moments, exerting her will over her feelings because she knew that in this instance, they were betraying her. She wanted more...but not really from that particular boy. Any boy would do and she knew this made it all wrong.

Now she felt the recognisable strong pull of sheer physical attraction to Paul Duret. She was intensely aware of the strong pressure of his hand holding her own; of the warm, rough feel of his cheek against hers; of the crisp, strange-smelling dark hair where his head touched her forehead. She was equally aware of his hurried breathing and even more so of the thudding of her own heart which she was sure he must feel against his chest since he was holding her tightly to him. One half of her longed to draw back from this intensity of feeling; afraid, yet not afraid; attracted and yet vaguely disturbed as if something deep within her subconsciousness was warning her that this was wrong.

The tune came to an end, releasing her momentarily from the spell. She drew away from him but almost at once, the music started up again and Paul tried to pull her back into his arms.

'Really, I ought not...' she said hesitantly. 'Luc...'

'Luc can easily find another partner if he wishes,' Paul said firmly, smiling. 'He knows everyone, very nearly. He can spare you to me for one more dance, I think.'

She could have refused but she knew she did not wish to do so. She allowed him to draw her back into his arms. This time, he made no attempt at conversation. They were dancing so close that it felt to Ann as if they had become one person. The floor was crowded and any serious movement became practically impossible so that they scarcely moved away from the one spot where they had begun to dance. She was aware that couples all around were clasped as she and Paul were clasped, as if in an embrace. A young couple close beside them were kissing. They seemed totally oblivious to the fact that anyone might be watching them. If they knew, they simply did not care.

Ann felt her heart lurch at the thought. She wouldn't care either, if Paul were to kiss her now. She wanted him to. She longed to know what it would be like to be kissed by him.

As if sensing the thoughts that were raging through her mind, Paul's arm tightened even closer around her. He let go of her hand, leaving his own free now to close gently around the back of her head. Unconsciously, she allowed her arm to encircle his waist. For a moment they stood thus, feet perfectly still, bodies swaying gently in time to the music. Ann felt as if she had turned to air, her body liquefying and moulding itself into her partner's.

The thudding of her heart was so violent, she found it difficult to breathe. But she knew she would not draw away. She wanted to stay here like this for ever and ever, floating in an incredible, beautiful dream.

Suddenly the tempo of the music changed and the group were playing a noisy pop tune. Paul released Ann and without asking her if she wished to continue dancing, led her off the floor.

'I think it best if I return you to Luc,' he said, guiding her back between the crowd of standing onlookers and groups of tables. 'He will be wondering what had become of you.'

Ann felt an irrational annoyance. It was as if Paul were relegating her to the nursery! Back to Nanny's care! She was not yet fully out of the dream quality of the last dance and it shook her a little to realise how perfectly at ease Paul seemed when her own legs were still trembling and her heart still thudded violently.

'Ah, so there you are!' Luc greeted her, standing up as Paul held out her chair for her to sit down. His eyes were unsmiling. Paul ignored him and bowed over Ann's hand, kissing it as he had done previously in the café bar. This time she knew she had not imagined that his lips lay longer than was justified against her skin.

'*Au revoir,*' Mademoiselle Ann. Thank you for the dance,' he said, and without a further word, turned away and left them.

'It is time we went home,' Luc announced into the silence that ensued.

Ann's head jerked upwards.

'Oh, no, Luc!' she cried involuntarily. 'I'm having so much fun!'

'It has passed midnight,' Luc replied gravely. 'You may remember I promised Maman we would not be late.'

With the greatest reluctance, Ann stood up, Luc could not know but she had hoped she might have another dance later with Paul. She mustn't blame him for wanting to leave now. She must recall that all this was very familiar and no doubt very dull for him. He could come here any night of his life. But then, so could she for the next year. The thought revived her flagging spirits.

Outside the night seemed even darker. The stars had disappeared and Luc looked up at the sky and said:

'I'm afraid it might not be such a fine day tomorrow. It is warmer and this is not a good omen for sunny weather.'

At first he did not, as on the way down, hold her arm, but when her foot slipped suddenly on an icy patch, he was beside her in an instant steadying her. She was grateful for his support.

They walked a little way in silence and then Luc said abruptly:

'Paul Duret is not a desirable friend for you, Ann.'

Ann's head jerked upwards. Her quick temper flared.

'Why do you say that?' she asked. 'What's wrong with him? He seemed very nice to me. His manners are perfect and he was extremely polite.'

'But naturally!' Luc's voice struck her as sarcastic, as if he set no store by such assets. 'All the same, it is best you do not make a friend of him, Ann.'

'Why not? What's wrong with him?'

70

Ann asked again. Suddenly, her heart jolted with dismay. 'He...he isn't married, is he?'

'No...not exactly!'

Ann frowned.

'What do you mean, not exactly? Is he engaged?'

'He is not formally engaged,' Luc answered with slow deliberation. 'Nevertheless, he does have...women friends...one in particular with whom he may one day marry.'

Ann felt her tense nerves relax. She actually laughed.

'Well, of course an attractive man of his age has friends of the opposite sex. It would be very unnatural if he did not, wouldn't it? Anyway, I don't see what all this has to do with my being friendly with him. I'm sure you are trying to be nice or kind or protective or something, but really, Luc, I'm quite old enough to choose my own friends.'

'Are you?' The words were out before Luc could stop them. He went on quickly: 'It is more difficult to select friends in a strange country,' he said. 'Please believe me, Ann, when I tell you not to take anything Paul Duret says with seriousness.

He...he has a very doubtful reputation.'

Ann digested this information in silence. Luc could not know it, but his words had added a further touch of excitement to the mystery he was creating around Paul Duret. Perhaps, she told herself, Paul was a flirt and had broken a few hearts in his day. If that were so, she would see to it that she did not take anything that happened between her and Paul seriously. She, too, could flirt. Their friendship could be very light-hearted and such fun!

But even as the thought went through her mind, she knew that she did not feel very light hearted about Paul; that the emotions aroused in her by their dancing had been anything but casual fun.

'Oh, nonsense, Ann,' she chided herself silently. 'It's just that he's very attractive and I'm at a loose end. It meant nothing at all—to him or to me.'

'Forget him, Luc,' she said aloud. 'After all, what possible harm is there in a dance, for heaven's sake? You take everything so seriously! You ought to be more superficial, like me.'

Luc did not reply and Ann felt disconcerted by his silence. It was as if he were deliberately refuting the idea of her being superficial. She felt impelled to elaborate.

'Look, I'm eighteen, nineteen next birthday. I'm not a child, Luc. If you're going to be worried every time I dance with a man who invites me, you're going to have an awfully tedious time taking me out. Please, Luc, don't be so serious about it. You make me feel I've spoilt your evening.'

'You mustn't think that, Ann. I have much enjoyed our evening, and especially the honour of being with you. I hope you will allow me very many times to take you dancing. I'm afraid it is I who spoilt your fun.'

Ann snuggled up closer to him, feeling happier.

'The trouble with you, Luc, is that you're much too nice!' she said. 'But please don't worry about me. My parents never do and even my brother James, says I've got my head screwed on the right way. He says it's screwed on so tight I won't let myself fall in love until a totally eligible young man comes along. Then only after I've worked out he'd make an ideal husband, I'll tell myself to fall in love with him and I will.'

Luc was following her words carefully.

He did not laugh as she anticipated.

'If it is truly what your brother thinks, then I do not believe he knows you very well,' he said quietly. 'I think you are a very impulsive person. Once I was this way, too, and now life had taught me to be different. But not so different that I cannot recognise in you what once was in me.'

Now it was Ann's turn to fall silent. She waited for Luc to continue but he said nothing more and she decided that this was not the moment to probe. If he wanted to tell her more about himself and what had changed him, he would have done so.

They reached the door of the chalet. Luc stood for a moment without opening it. His face, young and very serious, was looking directly at Ann's.

'At least tell me that you accept me as your friend,' he said.

'But of course I do!' Ann cried instantly. 'And I am your friend, too. You've no idea how happy I am to have found you here, Luc. It's like having an older, wiser, far more interesting James around to watch over me. I feel safe with you.'

Neither spoke the thought that crossed

both their minds as they stepped through the open door into the hallway. Ann might be safe with Luc but it was far less certain that she was safe from Paul Duret.

4

A week had passed since Ann's arrival in Aiguille. Her life had settled into a routine which kept her busy and was never dull. When she was not acting as waitress at the club, she was out on the ski slopes, either with Luc or practising alone.

Her letters home were ecstatic. The skiing bug, she wrote, had really got her in a big way. She was beginning to make progress and Luc had told her she was doing exceptionally well for a beginner. Luc had taken her several times dancing at the club in the evenings.

She mentioned Luc's name in every other sentence but never that of Paul Duret. It was a subconscious omission. She would not have known how to describe the strange relationship which seemed to be developing between them. Nothing was said that established there even was a relationship, yet Ann felt its existence and her life had assumed an extra dimension because of it.

Sitting in her bedroom, reading over her most recent letter home, she found herself on the point of mentioning Paul. She wanted to write his name and yet curiously, she could not. What, after all, could she say that would make sense to the family, back in England where life was so totally different? That Paul managed, somehow, to be where she was at least four or five times a day? That he was always at the club when she was working there and always at one of the tables for which she was responsible? That he always looked very directly into her eyes with a secret smile she was never quite sure if she had imagined or if it was normal for him to smile in such a way? That on three occasions, when she had been ski-ing on the nursery slopes alone, without Luc, he had 'run into her accidentally'. He usually had some simple explanation for being there—he wanted to talk to a particular ski instructor; weather conditions higher up the mountains were adverse for his ordinary ski-ing haunts. But she couldn't be absolutely sure if he had planned to see her or if these meetings really were accidental. This uncertainty both excited and confused her so that invariably she would find herself blushing when suddenly he would appear at her side with that strange smile and compelling voice saying:

'Ah, Mademoiselle Ann. How nice to see you!'

The words he spoke were polite, impersonal, yet the look in his eyes was anything but impersonal and Ann could not make it out. If he really were interested in her, why did he not ask her for a date? There was no reason she could see why he did not ask her to go dancing with him at the club one evening. Yet he had so far never suggested an assignation and seemed content to come to the table where she and Luc were seated and ask her for a dance as he had the first evening. Ann found herself waiting for him to appear, telling herself that this time, she would refuse to dance, just to see what happened. But she never did refuse, even though she was conscious of Luc's continued disapproval of her having anything to do with Paul. Usually Paul seemed to be alone. He would stand at the bar and whenever she glanced in his direction, she would find him staring at her so that she would give a quick, nervous smile and turn quickly away again. Above everything else, she did not want to appear to be looking for him but as the minutes went by, the temptation to glance round became too strong for her. It was almost as if he were willing her to look at him.

But last night Paul had not been alone. He was at a table with an older woman Ann judged to be in her forties. She was very chic in a beautifully cut navy blue crêpe trouser suit which clung to her short, rather rounded figure. Had she been less smartly dressed and coiffured, she might have looked matronly, for she tended to the plump side and her face was, if anything, rather plain. But she was perfectly made up and Ann was forced to admit that Paul's companion was very distinguished-looking if not at all beautiful.

For half an hour, she had restrained the impulse to ask Luc who Paul was with. Luc knew everyone and was certain to be able to tell her what she wanted to know. But her pride would not permit her to let Luc know she was in any way interested in the fact that Paul was with a partner. In the end, she did ask Luc who was the woman in the blue trouser suit, trying to make Luc believe that it was her clothes in which she, Ann, was interested.

Luc had glanced at Paul's table and his face tightening, said:

'That is Madame Verdos. She is a Parisienne and you are unlikely to see her ever looking anything but chic. She is a very wealthy woman and buys only from the smartest fashion houses.'

Ann was consumed with curiosity to know more but Luc did not proffer any further information and Ann could not bring herself to ask. She took it for granted that Paul would not invite her to dance but his companion went through to play boule and Paul came at once to their table to bow over her hand as usual.

As usual, despite her contrary wish to refuse him, she rose at once and preceded him onto the floor.

Paul smiled down at her as he took her into his arms.

'I was afraid that perhaps I would not have the pleasure of dancing with you this evening,' he said. 'As you may have noticed, I am not free to do as I wish this evening.'

There seemed nothing Ann could reply to this statement since she could not ask the obvious question 'Why are you with this woman? What is she to you?'

In silence she danced with Paul's arms holding her close, realising that silly as it might be, she was actually jealous. As if sensing her thoughts, Paul said:

'Madame Verdos is a very old friend of mine. She has just arrived from Paris so it would have been very ill mannered of me not to act as her escort this evening.'

Ann felt herself relaxing. She couldn't be certain but she was sure Paul was trying to reassure her that he was not in any way interested in his companion; that he would much prefer to be escorting her; dancing with her.

'Anyway,' she told herself with a lifting of her spirits, 'this Madame Verdos is far too old to interest a man of Paul's age. There must be at least ten years difference between them.'

Now, her pen poised above the letter home, she suddenly realised that whilst ten years had seemed an absurd difference when she considered Paul's interest in Madame Verdos, there were also ten years between her and Paul!

She sighed. It was quite different if the man were older than the girl. A man with an older woman—somehow that had a different implication.

Suddenly, the colour flared in Ann's cheeks. She might be young but she was not ignorant. She knew very well that it was possible for a man to have an affair with an older woman; that often such women were very rich and beautiful and amused themselves spending money on a younger attractive man who revived their youth for them. Was this the relationship between Madame Verdos and Paul? Was this why Luc was trying to warn her against Paul? It would be typical of Luc to have too much delicacy of feeling to put such an idea in her mind.

Ann drew another deeper sigh. If it were true, she wanted nothing more to do with Paul. The sooner she put him right out of her mind and forgot him, the better. What did he mean to her anyway? The whole situation was really absurd—a stupid romantic idea that existed only in her mind.

'But I didn't imagine the way he looks at me, hold me when he dances, watches me all the time,' she thought.

So what if Paul did find her attractive! So did Luc. Why, then create such a big thing of it all in her mind?

'Because,' she thought honestly, 'I find him attractive, too.' It was high time she took herself in hand and stopped behaving like a schoolgirl. She had herself told Luc it would be extraordinary if a man as good looking as Paul Duret did not have companions of the opposite sex. If he wished to be associated with this Madame Verdos, it was no concern of hers. She was not committed to Paul in any way and the sooner she forgot about him the better.

But it wasn't easy to forget him. He was so often in the same place where she was. She began to avoid her usual haunts—chose a different nursery slope for her afternoon ski practice and a new coffee bar for her mid-morning chocolate. She told Luc she was a bit bored with the club, working there all day, and asked if they could go somewhere different in the evening.

'But of course!' he said at once in his kindly, thoughtful way. 'We will go to the Go-Go. You will like it there!'

The atmosphere of the Go-Go was very similar to that of the club but there was, as Ann had hoped, no sign of Paul. She relaxed and prepared to enjoy her evening alone with Luc. He seemed in very good spirits and danced with her more often than usual. He laughed a lot and teased her and held her hand at the table.

'You're in a very good mood!' Ann said eventually, smiling at a joke he had made about the couple at the adjoining table.

'So I should be!' Luc said happily. 'I am out alone with the most attractive young lady in Aiguille, the envy of all the men present. I am happy and content.'

'Well, I like being with you, too,' Ann said. 'But I don't see why this evening is special. We've been out dancing alone together five times now. What's special about this evening?'

The smile on Luc's face faded. His eyes became serious.

'Because tonight we are *quite* alone!' he said. 'We do not have Paul Duret hovering over our table.'

His words were so unexpected that Ann nearly gasped with surprise. She knew that the colour was revealingly back in her cheeks and her eyes dropped down to her hands, away from Luc's direct glance.

'What nonsense!' she said as lightly as possible. 'Paul doesn't hover over our table as you put it. I only ever have one dance with him.'

'But it is enough!' Luc said flatly. 'I have noticed the way he holds you, the way he looks at you. I have noticed, too, the way you look at him. It is not good, Ann. I am happy that tonight you should have chosen to be some place where he is absent!'

Ann attempted a laugh. It was not very successful.

'I do believe you are jealous, Luc!' she said. 'And it's just ridiculous. I've no interest in Paul Duret or he in me. You've been imagining things.'

'Look at me and tell me you believe that!' Luc said. 'I would be very much happier if I thought you really meant it.'

'Well, of course I mean it!' Ann said quickly. 'If there were anything between Paul and me, we'd have been dating ages ago. He's never asked me out and even if he did, I don't suppose I'd go. What interest could I possibly have in a man of his age?'

'Age?' Luc repeated. 'What has that to do with it? Duret is a very attractive man. He has always appealed to women and he knows how to attract. I accept what you accuse me of. I am jealous. But I am also concerned for you, Ann. I do not wish you to be hurt and a man like Duret...' he broke off as if realising he had already said too much.

Ann fidgeted uncomfortably in her chair. She was disconcerted by Luc's seriousness. Somehow his admission that he was certain there was an attraction between her and Paul lessened her own doubts and made her realise her daydreams might be real after all. She had almost succeeded in convincing herself that she was imagining everything and now here was Luc, sane, sensible, nice Luc, telling her he had seen with his own eyes how things were between her and Paul.

'Luc, this really is absurd. Paul Duret means nothing to me nor I to him. I can't think what makes you believe otherwise. Why, you must have seen him the other evening with that Madame Verdos. It's fairly obvious he prefers older women. He wouldn't have any serious thoughts about a girl of my age. Why should he? I probably appear very gauche and unworldly to him.'

'And that could be exactly what attracts him!' Luc said. 'I, too, find your innocence attractive. Why should not he who no doubt is bored with dancing attendance upon poor Madame Verdos?'

'Poor? Why do you say that?' Ann asked, caught up in spite of herself by curiosity.

'Because she is a very unhappy woman. She is in love with Duret but he is not in love with her.'

'How can you possibly know such a thing?' Ann asked, almost angrily. 'And even if it's true, it isn't Paul's fault if he doesn't love her. Surely she must appreciate the difference in their ages?'

Luc drew in his breath sharply.

'I do not wish to disillusion you, Ann. As you say, how can I know except from hearsay. Gossip is never to be trusted. All the same, it is said that Duret has long pretended to love her and for a while, succeeded in making her believe it, too. Now he does not trouble to hide how he feels and she knows the truth but cannot live without him. That is why I say "poor" Madame Verdos. She is enslaved by a myth!'

Ann found relief in laughter.

'I never heard such a fairy tale!' she said. 'Nor did I realise what an idealist you are, Luc. I'm sure none of this is true. And even if it were, if Madame Verdos knows Paul no longer loves her, why should she continue to see him?'

'Ah, Ann, how young you are!' Luc said, as if he, himself, were an elderly man. 'She is in love with him. Do you not know that when one loves truly, one has no pride?'

Something resembling pain in Luc's voice caused Ann to look at him with new eyes.

'You sound as if you speak from experience,' she said gently. 'Have you been hurt, Luc? Is that why you are so afraid of involvement?'

Her guess was so near the mark that it was Luc's turn to be confused. He did not wish Ann to know about Ingeborg. He did not wish ever to have to remember that episode in his life—far less talk about it to someone else. Yet Ann's words were wise. He *was* afraid of involvement. He was afraid of loving her and yet he knew there was little he could do to stop himself from falling in love with her. In the brief week since she had come to his home, he had loved her a little more each day as he grew to know her better. He loved her gaiety and simplicity and youthful honesty. He liked her ability to be quiet and serious if the occasion required it, or to be enthusiastic and happy and eager as she was about her ski-ing. He liked the keen way she went about her work at the club and the thoughtful way in which she tried to help his mother at home. She was considerate and kind yet never dull or ingratiating. And withal, she was more attractive to him physically than any girl he had known since Ingeborg. In short, he loved her. And the more intense the love he felt, the more afraid he became of Paul Duret's interest in her. He could see exactly what the older man was doing—arousing Ann's curiosity and approaching her in a subtle, unobvious way that had already succeeded in intriguing her. A more direct, obvious approach might well have failed with someone like Ann who must be well used to the advances of the opposite sex. Duret, with his experience of women, would know that and had hit on just the right way to appeal to her romantic senses.

That she was a romantic at heart, Luc had little doubt. He couldn't bear it if she were hurt as he, himself, had been hurt and disillusioned. Yet his very desire to protect her had only made her more interested in Duret.

'Oh, do let's forget about Paul and enjoy

ourselves!' Ann was saying with simulated unconcern. 'And stop worrying about me, Luc. I promise you I'm quite well able to look after myself. After all, I *am* nearly nineteen.'

Despite himself, Luc smiled and took her back on the dance floor. For the rest of the evening Paul's name was not mentioned. But it appeared nonetheless, in Ann's private diary.

Did not see Paul today. Wonder if he is with M. Verdos? Luc warned me off yet again. Think L. might be a little in love with me. Must not encourage him as I only like him as a friend.'

The following day Ann was off duty. Luc had to go to Geneva with his father so she made her way early to the nursery slopes to practise the stem turns Luc had been teaching her yesterday. She made moderately good progress and arrived exhausted but content at the café-terrace at the top of the ski-lift. She was sitting in the sun sipping iced orange juice when an accented voice behind her asked permission to join her. It was Marie Jouer.

Surprised but pleased to see a familiar face, Ann removed her ski gloves and batons from the adjoining chair so that

Marie could sit down. She was wearing cyclamen coloured ski trousers with a white, navy and cyclamen coloured anorak. With her dark hair and complexion, the outfit was very becoming. Ann thought her more attractive than she recalled from their last brief meeting at the club.

'How are you enjoying your stay at Aiguille?' Marie asked. 'The Mentons are a charming family, are they not?'

For a few minutes Ann rhapsodised about life in general but Marie was not really interested in Ann's appreciation of the Swiss ski resort. She began to question Ann more closely about Luc.

'He's frightfully nice to me!' Ann replied innocently, at first unaware of the drift Marie's questioning was taking. 'He must get terribly bored messing around on the nursery slopes but he gives me a lesson every day. I think he must be a very unselfish person.'

'No doubt he is enjoying your company,' Marie returned. 'After all, you are very attractive. He might not be quite so kind to someone a little less pretty, shall we say?'

For the first time, Ann sensed something antagonistic in Marie's tone. The smile faded from her eyes.

'That's a funny thing to say about someone who's supposed to be a friend of yours,' she retorted spiritedly. 'I'm sure Luc is kind to everyone.'

'You are quick to defend him,' Marie replied. Her mouth was smiling but there was a hard speculative look in her eyes which did not escape Ann. She recalled her previous impression of Marie Jouer—that the young woman was more interested in Luc than he was in her. If Marie was in love with Luc, it would explain a lot of things.

'I'm very fond of Luc,' she said impulsively. 'But that's all there is to it. I think he's nice, attractive, fun to be with, but I'm not involved with him or intending to be. Was that what you wanted to know?'

For a moment Marie looked taken aback by Ann's directness. After the briefest pause, she suddenly smiled and said:

'Yes, as a matter of fact, that was just what I wanted to know. How clever of you to guess. I suppose it is always difficult for one woman to hide from another when she is in love. You will understand also, I'm sure, why I am a little jealous. You are very pretty and Luc spends so much time with you.' She laughed ruefully.

Ann smiled with genuine warmth.

'Well, now I know how *you* feel, I'll naturally try not to monopolise so much of Luc's time. I assure you he is just being nice. He's also trying to improve his English!'

Marie gave a slight shrug.

'It would be nice if that were all,' she said. 'But I am much afraid Luc finds pleasure in being with you. I think it is quite possible he could fall in love with you. Perhaps you will think I am greatly lacking in pride that I ask this favour of you, but if you do not have any personal interest in Luc, I would be very grateful that you should not encourage him to fall in love with you.'

Ann was momentarily silenced. It was a strange conversation to be having with a girl who was virtually a stranger. She was reminded of Luc's remark last evening—a woman really in love has no pride! Well, it was certainly true of Marie Jouer if she could approach her, Ann, on such a subject, asking her to leave Luc alone.

'I've no intention of encouraging Luc to fall in love with me,' she said honestly. 'It would be very awkward if he did so now that I am living with his family. I just want to be friends with him.'

She wished she could add that Luc was in any event far more interested in Marie, but she could not tell so blatant a lie. As far as she knew, Marie meant nothing more to him than an old friend. As it happened, Marie was thinking on the same lines. She said bitterly:

'I do not suppose it will make a lot of difference but I thank you anyway. You see, I have been in love with Luc for many years—since I was at school, in fact. But I know that he does not feel this way about me. Sooner or later I shall have to face up to the fact that he will love and marry some other girl but you are the first one in whom he has shown any real interest since Inge. I had begun to hope that maybe in the end, he would turn to me.'

'I'm sorry!' Ann said sincerely. 'Does he know how you feel?'

Marie smiled.

'Possibly. I don't know. One would imagine all the world would know but men can be very obtuse. They often do not see what they do not wish to see.'

'Perhaps if you were to tell him...' Ann began, but Marie broke in.

'For what purpose except to embarrass us both? He is not in love with me. If he cared even a little I should know at once. If I forced him to realise how I feel about him, he would break off our friendship altogether and then I would indeed be without hope. No, it is better I say nothing, do nothing, except wait. You are very kind, Mademoiselle, to wish to help me. I am glad I had the courage to approach you this morning. Believe me, I was afraid to do so. For all I could know, you wanted Luc for yourself and might have laughed in my face; or worse, laughed with Luc behind my back.'

'I'd never do that!' Ann cried. 'And please call me Ann. I'd like us to be friends.'

To her dismay, there were tears in Marie's eyes.

'I do not deserve to have you for a friend,' she said in a small, choked voice. 'But I wish it, too, so I'll confess that I did not approach you in a friendly spirit. I wished you harm. I would have done anything at all to hurt you if it would have helped to bring Luc closer to me. So you see, I don't deserve your friendship.'

96

'Oh, nonsense!' Ann said, partly embarrassed by this emotional confession, partly touched. 'You know, Marie, I've come to the conclusion that love isn't all it's cracked up to be. I mean, as far as I can see, it can be a horribly painful business if it's unrequited.'

Marie brushed away the tears and smiled.

'It is plain to see *you* are not in love,' she said. 'But I wonder how long you will remain immune. I know of someone who is quite crazy about you but you do not seem to care much for him. It is strange. Most women find him irresistible.'

'Him? Who are you talking about?' Ann asked, but the colour in her cheeks revealed she already knew the answer.

'Paul and I have talked a lot about you. He is not a man I like or admire but we have been allies this last week, trying to find a way to come between you and Luc.'

'Paul Duret!' Ann manged to repeat the name. 'But what interest can he possibly have in me? And anyway, there's nothing between Luc and me.'

Marie smiled.

'I know that now, but Paul thinks Luc

is mad about you and I was afraid *you* wanted *him*. So was Paul. As a friend, Ann, I think I owe it to you to warn you about Paul. He's not good. It would be best if you remain indifferent to him.'

'But I'm not...' Ann broke off. Until the words had sprung to her lips in impulsive denial, she had had no idea of their truth. But it was too late to retract. Marie was giving her a strange pitying look as she said softly:

'Poor Ann. So you're not, after all, immune. Well, be careful. Paul can be dangerous. Take my advice and avoid him before it is too late.'

'Too late? Too late for what?'

'Too late to prevent yourself falling in love.'

With a great effort of will, Ann managed to laugh.

'Why, Marie!' she said in a high bright little voice. 'As if I were likely ever to do such a silly thing as that!'

5

If Ann could have organised her life as she chose, she would have avoided seeing Paul Duret for at least a week; until such time as she could sort out the confusion of her feelings about him. She felt overwhelmed by the extraordinary rush of events which seemed to have overtaken her long before she was ready for them. First, there was Luc warning her against Paul. Then her own uncomfortable suspicions about his relationship with Madame Verdos. If Luc were right and Paul had been having an affair with the older woman, Ann did not wish to become involved. Now Marie Jouer had told her as a fact that Paul was a definite admirer of hers and jealous of Luc. He had even discussed with Marie how they could come between her and Luc.

One part of her mind considered the situation and found it both inexplicable and absurd. She barely knew Paul—had exchanged only the most formal conversation with him and danced with him half a dozen times. He'd never asked her out; never even asked her to have a drink with him. In fact, he'd given her no direct indication that he was in the least interested in her. Yet the other half of her mind was forced to admit that her own intuitions accepted Marie's statement. She felt Paul's interest in her. And just as strong, try though she might to ignore it, there existed her interest in him.

'Oh, bother it all!' Ann thought irritably as she laid the table in the Menton's dining room in preparation for their evening meal. 'I might as well admit I find him attractive. That doesn't mean I'm falling in love with him—or even that I like him. Both Marie and Luc say he is no good. Deep down, I'm inclined to agree. Far better to forget all about him!'

But in a closed, small community like that of Aiguille, it was virtually impossible to avoid seeing someone. Her job at the club necessitated her being there a large part of every day and Paul naturally was aware of this and could make a point of finding her whenever he chose to do so. He could also find her on the ski slopes if he cared to take the trouble. The nursery slopes were limited in length and he had only to go up and down a few times to be sure of catching sight of her. Short of telling him outright that she didn't wish to see him, she could not avoid meeting him.

'But I could avoid encouraging him!' Ann told herself in a moment of complete honesty. She knew that she had always responded to Paul's greetings when they met with a warm friendliness. Moreover, she had certainly not discouraged him from dancing so intimately with her.

'I didn't think there was any harm in it!' she argued with herself. 'A harmless flirtation—that's all.'

But it wasn't—and deep down she knew it. Paul might have been flirting with her but her responses to him had been involuntary.

Madame Menton came through from the kitchen with a tray of glasses.

'Luc and his father will be home soon,' she said with a warm glance of approval at Ann. 'It is quiet without them, no?'

Ann smiled back. She had become very fond of Madame Menton and wished quite suddenly that she could confide in her. As the older woman sat down for a moment to rest her feet, Ann toyed with the idea of questioning her about Paul. She was about to speak when Madame Menton said:

'Are you happy here with us, Ann?'

'Oh, yes, I am!' Ann cried sincerely. 'Everyone is so nice—Luc especially has been so kind and helpful. My ski-ing is really coming on well. By the way, I met Marie Jouer this morning. I believe she is a very old friend of your family.'

'Certainly! I was at school with Marie's mother and Marie and Luc have known each other since their cradle days. Once Madame Jouer and I hoped that one day Marie and Luc...but there, it never works out the way parents plan for their children. It is strange, though, that Marie has not yet married. Her parents would be happy to have a son-in-law. They would, I think, like to retire and hand over the hotel to Marie and her husband, if she had one. I ask myself sometimes if Marie is perhaps still a little in love with our Luc.'

'Perhaps!' Ann agreed, not wishing to betray Marie's confidence by being more emphatic. 'Perhaps, also, Luc will one day think again about marrying Marie?'

Madame Menton shrugged.

'I do not think so. Luc is a romantic. For him, it will have to be someone quite

102

new whom he can worship just a little. He knows Marie too well. Marie is self-willed and a little selfish, too. Luc needs someone less hard. And you, Ann? Is there no one special in your life? I think maybe you are still a little young to be thinking of marriage, no? First you need to learn a little about life.'

'Well, I'm certainly learning lots of new things here!' Ann replied smiling. 'It's all so very different from home. I suppose in one's own home, it's natural one should be treated as a child. Here I feel really grown-up.'

'Do not grow up too fast, *ma petite!*' Madame said gently. 'One is grown up so very much longer than one is a child. To be adult is to take on responsibilities; to have to become less selfish. Enjoy yourself a little longer as a *jeune fille.*'

'You talk like Mother!' Ann said half laughing. 'I don't know why parents always warn their children against growing up. I'm quite prepared to accept the disadvantages along with the advantages.'

'Youth is in such a hurry!' sighed Madame. 'So impatient. We have a proverb I find most meaningful, Ann. *"Qui rit Vendredi, Dimanche pleurera"*. I think in

English this would be translated: "Who laughs on Friday, will cry on Sunday". Such is life, I think.'

'But I do not think you are ever unhappy, Madame!' Ann said thoughtfully. 'In the week I have been here, I've never seen you cross or upset or anything but cheerful.'

Madame Menton smiled.

'That is because I have finished my growing up. I have a good husband, two good sons and a happy home. My way of life is settled and I am content. But for the young—they suffer. And we, their parents, cannot prevent it. My poor Luc...but there was nothing I could do. He had to find out for himself.'

She was talking more to herself than to Ann but Ann said softly:

'Marie Jouer mentioned a girl called Inge Luc had been in love with once. Was she the one who hurt him?'

Madame nodded.

'But he is over it now. For a long time I thought he would never get over his bitterness towards women. It makes me happy to see him so happy and gay in your company. You are good for him, Ann.'

'I like being with him,' Ann said, suddenly shy.

The conversation became more general, as they spoke of England and Madame translated young Pierre's first letter home. It seemed he was finding life at Ann's home as interesting and novel as she was finding life at Aiguille.

They were interrupted by the return of the two men of the household. Monsieur Menton had brought home a pot plant for his wife and Luc presented Ann with a beautiful box of Swiss chocolates.

'I shall get terribly fat if I eat them!' Ann thanked him.

'But you have no need to concern yourself with your figure!' said Monsieur Menton jovially. 'So thin, is she not, Luc?'

They all teased her for a while and then sat down to one of Madame's delicious savoury veal stews. The mood was festive and Ann felt herself relax, knowing she was accepted by them all now as a welcome addition to the family.

After supper Luc suggested they go along to dance for an hour or two. But Ann, unwilling to leave the warm closeness of the family circle for the uncertainty of meeting further emotional complications, told Luc she would rather have a quiet evening at home. He did not seem in the least disappointed and produced a chess board. Ann was given her first chess lesson, accompanied by much friendly advice from Monsieur Menton and a lot of friendly teasing from Luc. It was fun—childish fun when they began to accuse each other of cheating and Madame Menton, surveying them benignly, was forced to tell them to quieten their laugher or they would be hearing complaints from the neighbours.

At ten o'clock, Luc went to make coffee but his parents decided to retire to bed. She and Luc were left alone in front of the glowing red embers of the big marble stove. It was warm, friendly and intimate.

Ann sighed.

'It's been a lovely evening,' she said. 'I'm glad we didn't go dancing.'

'I, too!' said Luc, watching the warm golden shadows from the stove flickering across Ann's cheeks. All but one table lamp had been turned out by Madame Menton and the room was quiet and softened in the half light. He knelt down on the big rug where Ann was sitting on her heels staring into the fire, and gently put his arms round her from behind her back, reaching down the length of her sleeves to cover her bare hands with his own.

Ann felt herself drawn backwards so that the back of her head rested against Luc's shoulder, his face touching her hair. It was a strange position in which to be, but tired, sleepy and relaxed, it was wonderfully comfortable and comforting.

'Dear, nice Luc!' she murmured on a long sigh.

He was silent, saying nothing: she could not see his face but felt the slight pressure of his hands in response to her words.

They sat so for a few minutes and then Luc abruptly withdrew his arms and knelt up to reach for the coffee.

'It will be getting cold,' he said, handing her a cup and saucer. And then added: 'Once you said to me that you felt I was like an elder brother to you. Do you still feel this way, Ann?'

Surprised, she turned and looked at him over her shoulder.

'In a way, I suppose. But differently. I don't know, Luc. I mean, I suppose I know inside me that you aren't a brother. Anyway,' she smiled, 'it was meant as a compliment. I'm very fond of James.'

'Thank you. Nevertheless, I would prefer that you thought of me not as a brother!' His tone of voice was light but with an underlying seriousness.

'A friend, then!' Ann agreed. 'A very, very good friend.'

It suddenly occurred to her that the atmosphere was more attuned to romance than friendship. Something in Luc's eyes warned her that given the slightest encouragement, he might try to kiss her. She recalled her promise to Marie and said quickly:

'I met another friend of yours today, Luc—Marie Jouer. She and I have become friends, too.'

'Marie?' Luc seemed surprised. 'Well, that is nice for you both.'

'You don't sound particularly convinced!' Ann said teasingly. 'Don't you believe girls can become as close friends as girls and boys?'

'But of course—in some circumstances. But Marie...' he broke off, obviously unwilling to be disloyal to his childhood companion.

'You mean because she is specially fond of you?' Ann probed gently.

'Well, yes!' Luc replied awkwardly. 'I

always have the discomfort of feeling with Marie that she expected I would propose to and eventually marry her. Of course, I may be quite wrong but we were both aware our parents wished it.'

'But you do not?'

'I am not nor ever will be in love with Marie.' It was a statement of fact which did not bode well for Marie's future happiness, Ann thought.

'And Marie?' she asked. Although she knew the true answer, she wanted to discover Luc's view of the matter.

'Well, it is difficult to be sure. I think it may be just an idea she has in her head since childhood—one she cannot bring herself to relinquish. But she can be rather...well, possessive? If I have taken out other girls, as occasionally I have done here in Aiguille, Marie has somehow found a way of exhibiting her displeasure. Not to me—but to the girls I have escorted. That is why I was surprised to know she had invited you to be her friend. I...I would have expected rather the contrary.'

So Luc was not as blind to the true state of affairs as he might seem, Ann thought.

'Poor Marie!' she said, more to herself

than to Luc. 'It must hurt her very much that you don't love her if she loves you. Don't you think that one day...?'

'No!' Luc interrupted with a forcefulness that was unnecessary. 'Marie knows this, too. The sooner she accepts this as the truth, the easier it will be for us both. I do not wish to seem hard but I see no point in encouraging Marie to expect or hope that I will change in this respect.'

'But you might change!' Ann argued. 'How can you be so sure?'

This time Luc met and held her eyes. To her dismay, he said flatly:

'For one thing, because of the way I feel about you. If I felt anything at all about Marie, I could not entertain the emotions I have for you. Now, have I offended you?'

'No, of course not, but...' Ann stared back at him unhappily. Without intending to, she had precipitated Luc into saying more than he had meant to say, certainly more than she had expected to hear. 'But however you feel about me, Luc...don't please, let's get serious. I'm not ready to be serious about my life yet. I just want to enjoy myself—have a good time. Can't we just be good friends the way we mentioned earlier?'

110

'Of course!' Luc agreed. 'But that will not prevent me from hoping that one day your feelings for me will grow to be something deeper. I will not speak of love for we have not known each other long enough to be able to be sure about so important a matter. But we will talk of it again—when we know each other better. Until then, I am more than happy to be the "good friend" you desire.'

'But, Luc, I don't feel as you do. I'm not even sure if I know what love is. I wouldn't want you to think...'

'I expect nothing from you, Ann. Forget even that I mentioned my feelings for you. I am not worried. I shall not be worried until you tell me that you think you are in love with someone else! Until then, I am more than content to be able to be with you each day in friendship. I beg you now to forget this conversation. I shall forget it also.'

Ann let the matter drop. Clearly, Luc had not meant to reveal himself so far. It was no doubt due to the mood, the intimacy of the room and the fact that they were both relaxed and not on guard. Maybe he didn't even mean what he had said.

She finished her coffee and stood up, announcing her intention of going to bed. 'Yes!' agreed Luc. 'I, too, am tired!'

But he reached out a hand to detain her and before Ann could anticipate his intentions, pulled her into his arms and kissed her on the mouth. It was very much a lover's kiss and for a moment, Ann's senses were stirred. She liked Luc, found him attractive. There was no reason why he shouldn't kiss her—yet even as she felt herself responding, she knew that this was not fair. Luc was expressing more than an easy-going friendship in his kiss. She could not use him for a few moments of casual sensual enjoyment. Moreover, she knew that it wasn't really Luc's lips she wanted against her own; Luc's arms encircling, Luc's voice whispering endearments to her. What she really wanted—the man she really wanted—was Paul Duret.

6

When Ann woke next morning, her mind was made up. She was not going to give Paul Duret another thought. Luc and Marie would not have warned her against him without good cause. It was ridiculous to waste so much time thinking about him.

This decision, firmly made, seemed to lift a weight off her mind and she joined the other three members of the household feeling happy and vaguely relieved as she sat down to a breakfast of hot chocolate, croissants and apricot jam.

Luc took her for a ski-ing lesson immediately after Ann had completed her share of the housework. He was very complimentary about the progress Ann had made with her stem turns and told her that if she kept up this rate of achievement, he'd have her off the nursery slopes and onto the more advanced runs before he had to leave Aiguille to start work in Geneva.

'Only a few more weeks!' he said

regretfully. 'I was looking forward to it but now I know I shall miss all this very much.'

Both knew that he really meant he would miss Ann. She teased him out of his momentary despondency, reminding him he would be back most weekends. The thought cheered him up at once.

Luc's father wanted him later in the morning for some business transactions at their bank, so they parted company at mid-day. Ann went off to change into her working clothes ready for when the pre-lunch crowd descended on the club for drinks.

She was, as usual, kept very busy. There was, as always, an Italian family with three small children who turned up every day at one of her tables for a spaghetti lunch. Innumerable skiers wanted a 'Curling'—a long, brandy-based drink which was very popular and no doubt thirst quenching. Others wanted coffee, chocolate, cold soft drinks and snacks.

Most of the requests were familiar to Ann now and she was proud of her progress in French. It was rare for her to have to ask one of the other waiters to translate an order for her. One or two faces were already familiar to her and those she recognised greeted her with friendly warmth. She caught sight of Marie and waved to her. Two of the ski instructors ordered drinks and tried to detain her talking but she was too busy to stay chatting to them and moved off to the bar to collect another tray of drinks.

Paul Duret touched her arm.

'Mademoiselle Ann. *Bon jour!*'

As usual, the unexpectedness of his voice startled and confused her. She attempted to stop the hot colour rushing into her cheeks but did not succeed.

'I can't stay and talk. I'm very busy!' she said defensively.

'I know. I can see. But this afternoon you will not be on duty. I wondered if you would give me the pleasure of letting me take you up to *le Point?*'

Ann was drawn into conversation. She had forgotten her waking intentions to forget all about this man.

'The Point? But you know I couldn't ski up there!'

Paul Duret smiled.

'Not to ski—to admire the magnificent view. It is a perfect day with no mist or fog and very warm. I think you would enjoy it.

You have not yet been, no?'

Ann shook her head, biting her lip. She meant to say no to the suggestion but she was very tempted to say 'yes'. She knew there was a café restaurant on top of the mountain where they could sit in the sun. Luc and Madame Menton had both extolled the beautiful view. What reason had she to refuse?

'You have other plans?' Paul was asking her gently. 'I do hope not for it would give me the greatest pleasure if you would accompany me.'

For another long moment Ann hesitated. How was she to tell Luc at lunch time that she would not be ski-ing with him in the afternoon? Besides, he had himself suggested taking her up to the Point to see the view next weekend. Madame Menton enjoyed an occasional ride up there in the cable car and they were all going together.

'But I'm not answerable to Luc for what I do!' she thought, suddenly annoyed with herself and with Luc for the feeling that she was obliged to him in some way. 'If I choose to go with Paul Duret...'

'You *will* come with me?'

She looked up and met the penetrating

gaze of Paul's blue eyes. Once again, the colour rushed into her cheeks.

'All right!' she stammered, both awkward and ungracious in her confusion. 'What time?'

'Shall we say half past two? At the bottom of the cable car lift?'

Now that the decision was made, Ann felt anxious and extremely annoyed with herself for her own weakness. Only a few hours ago she had made up her mind to remove all thought of Paul firmly from her mind. Yet here she was, committed to spending an afternoon with him. It was really ridiculous. Moreover, what *could* she say to Luc? He wouldn't like it. She knew it instinctively.

Ann had never thought of herself as a coward but now she knew she would do anything to avoid having to tell Luc she had made a date with Paul. The more she thought about it, the less she wanted to tell him.

The Mentons came into lunch, Luc with them. He waved and smiled at Ann and she found herself avoiding his eyes. When at last she was free to sit down and join them at their tables, she was unusually quiet and reserved. Luc noticed at once.

'Something wrong, Ann?' he asked solicitously. 'Don't you feel well?'

'Oh, I'm fine!' Ann replied. But Luc's words had given her the excuse she had unconsciously been desiring. 'I'm a bit tired. I don't think I'll ski this afternoon. Do you mind, Luc?'

'But of course not!' he said. 'We'll sit on the balcony in the sun and take it easy.'

Ann felt the tell-tale colour warming her cheeks.

'I thought I...I'd do some shopping—get my hair cut, perhaps...' The lies came out with great difficulty. Madame Menton rescued her.

'You must not monopolise Ann's free time,' she said, wagging a finger reproachfully at her son. 'Women have other things to do besides waste their time in the company of young men.'

It was Luc's turn to look embarrassed.

'Forgive me, Ann,' he said. 'I didn't mean to impose my company on you.'

Her guilt increased with his obvious embarrassment. It was on the edge of her thoughts to find a way to tell Paul Duret she would not go with him after all, but suddenly Monsieur Menton said:

'It is just as well. I need Luc's help with

my accounts. This afternoon would suit me very well to get down to work, eh, Luc?'

For the remainder of the meal, Ann tried to make normal conversation. But her mind was elsewhere. She felt miserable for deceiving Luc—lying to him about her proposed afternoon activities. She was naturally a very honest person and she hated herself for the lie, even though she knew it had partly been made to save Luc anxiety on her behalf. Because he was partly the cause of her guilt, she answered sharply when he spoke to her and Luc's face became withdrawn and unhappy. Ann disliked herself even more.

'I wish Paul hadn't asked me!' she thought violently. But she knew that was a lie, too. Deep, deep down, her heart was thudding with excitement in anticipation of the afternoon to come.

★ ★ ★ ★

Ann was quite unprepared for the changed Paul who greeted her at the cable car lift. A small queue of skiers had formed awaiting their turn to get into the little two-seater cabins. As she joined him at the end of the queue, Paul linked his arm through hers as if they were the very oldest, closest of friends, and kissed her cheek.

'How very beautiful you look!' he said. 'And how very charming when you turn so pink! Do I embarrass you? You must not be ill at ease with me.'

'I'm not!' Ann heard herself say childishly. But she felt very unsure of herself; unsure of him, too, in this new possessive guise.

'I assure you, Ann, you have nothing to fear from me. Has someone been warning you against me? Telling you I am a rogue? That you cannot trust me?'

His words, though spoken semi-humorously, were too near the truth for Ann to reply with a smile. Watching her face, Paul added swiftly:

'I see that they have. Well, you must judge for yourself, Ann, what kind of man I am. It would not be fair for you to judge me on gossip alone.'

'But why should I judge you at all?' Ann asked, as they climbed the last few steps to the head of the queue. The conversation had become far too personal for her liking.

'Because all women judge the men in

their lives!' Paul said. 'Tell me honestly, Ann, have you not been judging me secretly? Wondering what I am really like? What it would be like to know me better?'

Her silence gave him his answer. He laughed and pressed her arm closer against him. She was very conscious of the gesture although it seemed to be quite natural to him.

'And I, too, have been thinking about you, my little English Miss. So young, so charming, so pretty.'

'I'm not all that young!' Ann cried, indignation making her speak naturally for the first time. 'I'm nearly nineteen, you know.'

Paul nodded.

'Yes, Marie told me!'

His expression was serious but his eyes were smiling. At last, Ann felt herself relax a little. She, too, smiled.

'Marie did not tell me *your* age,' she said.

'I am thirty-three—an old man compared to you! Tell me, Ann, how did young Luc react to your accompanying me this afternoon?'

Ann felt herself blushing again.

'As a matter of fact, I didn't tell him!' she said, with an attempt at nonchalance. 'I don't have to report my whereabouts to Luc, you know.'

'Miss Independence!' Paul teased her. 'Nevertheless, I have the impression Menton would not be very pleased if he did know you were with me. He doesn't approve of me.'

Paul's words were blunt and vaguely disturbing to Ann. She wasn't quite sure if he were being disparaging about Luc or about himself. But there was no chance to take the conversation further for it was their turn to climb into one of the little vacant cabins. There was not much room inside and she was conscious of the pressure of Paul's body against her as they sat side by side. Two skiers, with their batons, squeezed in opposite them and with a rush, the cabin swung off and up on the first stage of its climb.

Ann was fascinated as they hung first at treetop level and then fifty feet or more above the mountain side. Below, the skiers were like tiny ants weaving down the steep slopes. The sun was blazing in through the closed window and thoughtfully, Paul leaned across her and opened it so that a rush of icy cold air cooled her cheeks.

As they climbed still higher, the view became increasingly panoramic and fantastic. Snow-capped mountain peaks sparkled in the sunshine from across the valley below. The glare from the sun on the snow was dazzling and Ann was glad of her dark glasses.

They swung upwards over a small forest of green pine trees. Paul explained that one of the mountain ski runs passed through the wood. In icy conditions, it could be quite perilous to the less advanced skier.

Soon they were high above the tree level and Ann could see nothing but snow, the tiny dots of the skiers descending in what almost seemed slow motion. The sky was a brilliant azure blue.

'It's magnificent!' She breathed the words almost reverently. 'I had no idea there would be such a view as this. To think that I have been in Aiguille a whole week and never knew this existed!'

Paul nodded.

'For those who love the mountains, there is nothing else in the world to touch them on a day like this. The ski-ing conditions are perfect, too. One day I will take you down that run.'

Ann turned to him, eyes sparkling with excitement.

'Do you really think I could, Paul? I have a whole year in which to learn to ski well. I don't think I could go back to England happily now if I hadn't tried this "run" if only once!'

'Of course you will do it,' Paul said. 'As with everything else in life, the will is most important of all. If you wish for anything deeply enough, it will happen.'

His words were ambiguous but Ann was too immersed in the view to pause to question his ulterior meaning—if, indeed, there had been one.

They stopped at the halfway stage and a number of skiers dismounted, including the occupants of their cabin. Then they were off again, swaying slightly in the breeze, climbing towards the blue sky.

Paul covered Ann's ungloved hand with his and said gently:

'You are happy?'

She nodded, suddenly so happy that she wanted to sing aloud. She told Paul so and he laughed and agreed that maybe this was the spirit that moved mountain people to yodel on the mountain tops.

Before long, the cabin swung into the

shed where the passengers disembarked. Those few who were not descending on skis or had tired of the view from the restaurant, re-embarked for the descent.

Ann followed Paul out of the shed into the sunshine and along the path to the adjoining restaurant. There were literally hundreds of people sitting at the tables or lying on sun chairs, talking, drinking, laughing or suntanning. Some were fastening their skis ready for the run down. Others, just arrived, like she and Paul, were searching for a chair in the sun.

Miraculously, Paul found a couple of vacant deck chairs on the terrace from where Ann would be able to watch the skiers depart. The sun was high in the cloudless blue sky, very hot and shining directly upon them.

'It's wonderful—beautiful!' she cried.

At Paul's suggestion she removed her anorak. It was quite warm enough to be coatless despite the intense sharp cold of the air at that height. She breathed in deeply and her breath came out again like a cloud of steam.

'It's one of the things which always surprises me out here,' she told Paul.

'That it can be so cold and so hot at once!'

Paul watched the girl beside him thoughtfully. He was not yet ready to tell her that one of the most enchanting assets she possessed was her childish enthusiasm for everything. The Point was certainly anything but new to him but it was as if he were re-experiencing it all for the first time. He thought of his afternoons here with Yvonne Verdos. So often she was complaining because their chairs were wrongly positioned to the sun; because there was a draught round her legs; because the people nearby were talking too loudly or the waitress was taking too long to serve them with their drinks. Yvonne, like himself, was spoilt. They had done it all too often to see it with the fresh, untarnished gaze of this eighteen-year-old girl. He enjoyed these holidays in Aiguille; enjoyed the ski-ing and the carefree life of the resort, but it was all too familiar to be able to spark his imagination with the radiant excitement he could see in Ann's eyes. Through her, he was taking a new vision of the world around him.

'Brandy?' he asked her. 'Or would you prefer coffee?'

'Could I have hot chocolate?' Ann asked innocently. 'I know it isn't long since I had lunch, but I could drink chocolate till the cows come home. If I'm not careful, I shall get fat.'

Paul smiled ruefully. He certainly had no intention of admitting it, but even if he liked the thick sweet drink Ann preferred, he dared not drink it. He had to watch his figure even if she did not. Already he was beginning to notice a thickening of the hips and there was a suspicion of a jowl to his jaw. He had a dread of looking middle-aged, only outweighed by his dread of actually being so. His build was stocky rather than tall and thin and if he wished to retain his boyish appearance, he knew he must not indulge in fattening foods. The alcohol he consumed was bad enough.

He felt suddenly depressed. He had never, in his young manhood, appealed to girls like Ann. Somehow, his appeal had always been to older women. It was only in recent years that he had been able to attract girls as well as women and he knew this was due to his mental approach rather than to his physical appearance. He knew women and their foibles so well—had studied them so thoroughly—that he reckoned he could type them almost upon introduction; that he could seduce any woman by a technique which he skilfully varied according to their type. He had seldom been wrong in these judgements and seldom failed to make a conquest when he wanted.

He was both cynical about the opposite sex now and jaded in his appetite for conquest. Whilst he continued to make such conquests, it was only for the reassurance to his ego; the satisfaction demanded by his vanity. He no longer found pleasure in the women themselves. But with Ann, it was somehow different; he felt like a young man setting out to try to win a woman's love. Her youth, her innocence, her freshness intoxicated him in a way he had thought no longer possible.

Because of this special interest in her, he had forced himself to play his hand far more cautiously than he might have done with a girl who meant less to him. He planned his campaign thoughtfully and with care; deciding to arouse her interest by less obvious tactics than those she might be used to with young men of her own age group. The occasional accidental meeting, the odd glance, smile and subtle flirtation were alternated with the intensity of emotion he permitted when they had their once-nightly dance together. In this way, he had succeeded in arousing her interest. He was well aware now that she was fascinated by him, unsure of and a little afraid of him.

He wondered suddenly if Luc had told her about his association with Yvonne Verdos. He hoped not. He could not see a girl as young as Ann accepting happily the fact that he had a mistress. But he doubted that Luc had told her. If he were wise, he would find a way to do so himself before Luc did speak out and perhaps turn Ann against him. Luc certainly would speak out if he knew Paul had serious intentions towards Ann. Perhaps, this afternoon, he would discover a way to tell her the facts, so colouring the details that she could accept them without rejecting him.

Paul felt ill at ease. He was not used to coveting the good opinion of the women in his life. This need to respect Ann both irritated and intrigued him. She was not just any girl on holiday he could seduce and amuse himself with at will. She was different—and he was astute enough to realise it.

Paul did not yet fully understand his own feelings towards her. He wanted her—and he knew it would not be an easy conquest. Why then bother at all? What he did not yet know was that for the first time in his life, he, Paul Duret, was falling in love.

7

Yvonne Verdos lay on the balcony of her apartment, her face and arms heavily oiled, her closed eyes covered with little pads of cotton wool to protect her lids from the rays of the sun.

Beside her, on a deck chair, sat her friend and contemporary, a woman of Polish extraction, called Monika Jerski. Both women wore open-necked shirts, sleeves rolled up to absorb the maximum sunshine.

'It is almost hot enough to be in bathing costumes!' remarked Monika, a petite blonde woman, as she adjusted her sunglasses and with one of her quick rather nervous gestures, lit a cigarette.

'I do not hanker after a swim suit!' said Yvonne Verdos with a wry smile. 'I am no longer of the age...'

'Oh, nonsense, Yvonne!' her friend broke in. 'You still have an excellent figure.'

'Clothed, maybe. Otherwise...I am show-ing signs of my age, Monika, and even more am I feeling old.'

Something in the bitter tone of her voice caused her companion to look at her sharply. Yvonne's eyes were covered so that she could not read their expression.

'Paul?' she asked simply.

'Ah, Paul!' agreed Yvonne. 'There are days, such as today, when I wish I had never met him.'

There was so much sadness in her voice that again Monika gave her a sharp anxious glance.

'What has he done to hurt you this time?' she questioned with the familiarity of an old friend and confidant.

'Nothing—yet!' said Yvonne dryly. 'But I can see it coming, Monika. The symptoms are much as usual and though I might try not to see them, I recognise them none the less.'

'But you have so often told me, Yvonne, you can rise above Paul's little unfaithfulnesses. You have told me that you are willing to close your eyes so long as he does not leave you. Only last Christmas you said to me: "Monika, Paul has a new one—a little actress. But he will get over it as always. It is not serious".'

For a moment the woman on the sun

chaise remained motionless. Only the fingers of one hand, playing restlessly with a button on her shirt, revealed the inner tension.

'This time it is not "a little actress". This time...it *could* be more serious, Monika.'

Her friend laughed. The sound had in it a tinge of uncertainty.

'But why should you say that? Paul has had a dozen or more little affairs. They never do last. He always comes back.'

'That is what I tell myself. Each time I am a little more afraid that this time, perhaps, he will not do so. We cowards die a thousand deaths, Monika, before we face death itself. Who was it said that? It is so painfully true!'

'But you must not talk this way, Yvonne. It is not like you. You have so much courage. Paul will never leave you—I'm sure of it!'

'I wish I had your conviction,' said Yvonne Verdos on a long sigh. 'I am not blind or stupid, Monika. I am getting old. I feel it and I look it. Paul is in his prime. Other women are attracted to him. Why should he remain my lover?'

'You have more to offer him than most women!' Monika said carefully. 'You have given him so much over the years. He cannot forget all you have done for him.'

'Oh, my dear!' cried Yvonne as if the words hurt her. 'Don't you know that gratitude is one of the hardest things to live with? Paul may be grateful but the need for his gratitude must make him resent me bitterly. I know that.'

For a moment the two women remained silent. Then Monika said slowly:

'Paul knows that you love him—really love him. In the last resort, that must flatter him. After all, Yvonne, you are one of the few women who know *all* about him yet continue to love him, to accept him as an equal.'

'And don't you imagine that he resents that, too? I, alone, know he was once just a penniless gamin, roaming the slums of Paris without even enough to eat. When I met him, he was an out-of-work actor, with nothing but his looks and ambitions. I gave him the social education he wanted. Being a natural actor, he learned quickly and now he can comport himself in any company with total panache; without one being able to guess his origins. Because I love him, his background is not important to me but it is to Paul. He would prefer to forget he was ever other than he is now. Perhaps, with me, he know it is useless to pretend and though I never refer to the past, it is possible he thinks I remember it and hates me a little for knowing the truth.'

Monika digested this revelation with mixed feelings. Most people knew that Paul was once an actor but none, as far as she knew, were aware of his humble origins. It explained a great deal about Paul—about Yvonne Verdos' relationship with him, too.

Suddenly, Yvonne sat up, removing the cotton wool eye pads, and looked directly across at her companion.

'I can trust you, Monika, not to repeat any of this to anyone—ever? Paul would never forgive me for speaking of it. I don't know what made me do so except that I was feeling a little sorry for myself. I was off guard.'

'But of course you can trust me!' Monika said sincerely. She could well understand Yvonne's feelings. Obviously Paul would be very bitter about such indiscreet disclosures. 'Do not worry yourself on that score, Yvonne. I am not a tattler, especially in such matters. Besides, I am far too fond of you to wish you harm.'

They smiled at one another with a new warmth. They did not see a great deal of one another although both lived in Paris and met at social functions. They usually wrote to one another prior to the ski-ing season to arrange to be at Aiguille at the same time. The friendship might have been closer but for the fact that Moniker's husband disliked Paul and Yvonne seldom went to parties without him. Their liaison was known and accepted in their society but although many of Yvonne's friends tolerated Paul for her sake, few of the men did in fact, like him.

'Paul has taken the young English girl up to the Point this afternoon,' Yvonne said with an apparent nonchalance which did not deceive Monika. 'It is the first time he has taken her out alone.'

'The English girl? You mean the tall, slim young house guest of the Mentons?'

Yvonne nodded.

'But surely you have nothing to worry about in that direction? I only remarked to my husband last night that she and Luc Menton are seldom apart and it could well become the romance of the season.'

'I think any romantic notions belong

136

only to Luc. Mademoiselle Ann Elgar is heart free; very, very young and very, very pretty. Paul is much *épris*.'

'Even if your fears are justified, Yvonne, it will not be anything serious. A short affair, perhaps, and then...'

'I do not think our English Miss would be interested in "a short affair". I do not think she is what we would call "that sort of girl". Even in these days, Monika, it is possible to distinguish one type from another. There are still those girls a man wishes to take to bed and those he wishes to marry. I think Mademoiselle Elgar is a young lady who would expect a proposal if she fell in love.'

Monika gasped.

'You are not seriously suggesting Paul might wish to marry this girl?'

For the first time, Yvonne Verdos' taut face relaxed into a smile.

'No, indeed! I cannot see Paul marrying anyone. You know how he feels about being tied.'

Monika was one of the few people who knew that Yvonne would have married Paul herself had he been willing to marry her. A lot of their friends guessed as much but Monika knew the facts. Yvonne, a very wealthy woman, had a great deal more than just love to offer Paul. Far younger than she, he would live to inherit her private fortune.

Monika did not like Paul Duret. Although she, in company with most women, could appreciate that he was attractive, she could see him for exactly what he was—a near gigolo who used and abused poor Yvonne. He knew exactly how far he could go—how much her great love for him would tolerate in the way of affairs. Always, when Yvonne's near unlimited patience was exhausted, he would return, repentant, affectionate, lavishing attentions upon her, the attendant lover once more. As Monika had once said to her husband, 'To put it crudely, Paul knows on which side his bread is buttered.'

Monika had been vaguely surprised to learn that Yvonne was prepared to marry Paul. He was not, after all, an acceptable husband. At the same time, she was woman enough to understand Yvonne's need to tie Paul with unbreakable bonds; to attain security for her old age. But what really surprised her was that Paul was unwilling to sell his freedom, even though he stood to gain financial security for life. She could not believe his motives in rejecting marriage were altruistic. If he had turned Yvonne down, vast fortune with it, there had to be a good reason. Many a time Monika had wondered what it might be. Her husband said caustically that Paul was probably getting all the cash he needed and his freedom as well, so why tie himself down for life to a woman so much older?

Suddenly Yvonne leant over and patted Monika's hand as if it were her friend and not herself who needed comforting.

'Do not look so worried for me, Monika. If Paul *is* really interested in the girl, it won't last. It simply means that I may have to wait much longer than usual for him to get over it. Such affairs normally burn themselves out in a week or two once the "hunting" stage is over and Paul knows the woman is his for the taking. That is when his interest wanes. Since I doubt this time he will get what he wants, his interest is likely to wane that much more slowly.'

Monika sighed.

'I wish you'd give Paul up, Yvonne. It is all wrong that a woman of your age, your standing, your intelligence, should have to endure this. I hate to see you...'

'Humble myself?' Yvonne put in bitterly.

'Oh, don't think I like the situation, Monika. There are times when I rail at myself for not having more pride. But it is far too late for pride. I love Paul and he knows it and I could not retract that love—not now. I could only give Paul up for his own good; if he genuinely fell in love with a girl and wanted to marry her.'

'I doubt if Paul is capable of love in the sense you mean!' Monika said with more frankness than tact. But Yvonne did not take offence.

'I dare say you are right. But he can be very, very charming. There are times when we are together happily, when he makes all this anguish worth while the enduring. It is for those times I live, Monika.'

To her friend, Yvonne's situation seemed a tragic and unhappy one. Yet even she had to admit that she had seen Yvonne radiantly happy. Nevertheless, she could not herself believe that the relationship could be worth while. No doubt it was the natural consequence of Yvonne's earlier life. Her family had married her at the tender age of seventeen, fresh from her convent school, to a man twenty years her senior, whom she barely knew. It was a good marriage in the sense that Jean Verdos was a wealthy man of excellent family but from Yvonne's point of view, disastrous. He was a cold, highly intellectual perfectionist who had little or nothing in common with the romantic, warm-hearted, starry-eyed young girl he married. Their honeymoon was the end of Yvonne's dreams, not the beginning of a new life. Her husband was almost Victorian in his outlook and, indeed, his choice of so young and inexperienced a girl had been an unconscious insurance that he would be the controller, the dictator, the authority in his marriage. Yvonne was physically beautiful and intelligent. She soon learned to entertain for him as he wished, to run his big Paris apartment efficiently and effortlessly and this was really all he required of his wife. She was a business asset.

Perhaps fortunately for Yvonne, Jean Verdos died not ten years later, leaving her a rich young widow, still very attractive. But he had ruined her romantic ideals to such an extent that she could never find herself in the least attracted to men such as Jean who, now that she was a widow, came to call upon her. She had long ago encased herself in an artificial shell of cool, sophisticated irony. Now she merely laughed at the protestations of devotion and love that came her way.

But Paul, so totally different in every possible way but one from her former husband, managed to break down that barrier with his complete imperviousness to her *'grande dame'* manner. With his shrewd understanding of women, he attacked her inner senses with a gay bravado that at first amused then intrigued and finally won her.

Paul's only likeness to Jean, his physical, social and intellectual opposite, lay in his intense appreciation of money. Jean had always had it and meant to increase his fortune. Paul had never had it and with the same cool determination, sought to make his fortune.

Yvonne was by now old enough and cynical enough to see this for herself that where deviousness on Paul's part as to his motives might have helped her to withstand the physical attraction he had for her, his complete honesty with regard to his 'using' her, broke down her resistance and endeared him to her.

It was only after she had finally fallen in love with him, after he had become her lover, that his interest in her money and her social position began to hurt whenever she permitted herself to think about it. Always razor sharp in his astuteness, Paul saw this change of mood and changed his approach accordingly. He professed love and dependence upon her as a woman, telling her that even if she were penniless, he would feel the same way about her. She let herself believe him because it had become necessary for her to believe him. She was blindly, totally and helplessly in love with him—the way, as a convent schoolgirl, she had once genuinely believed she would love the man she married.

The fact that Yvonne had lived so many years without love only added fuel to the flames of this late flowering of her true self. Passion was twenty times the stronger for having been so long submerged.

But such blind devotion could not last when centred on so worthless, shiftless and selfish a man as Paul Duret. Little by little, Yvonne was forced to discover his true worth, to be hurt again and again, each time humbling her pride another degree as she forgave him his infidelities and occasional cruelties when his guard slipped.

Now, finally, she had reached a point

where nearly all her illusions were gone, all her pride but never, never all her love. That alone had endured and sustained her. She could not now envisage a life in which there was no Paul to love; to worry about, to wait for, to forgive, to be happy with in the moments when he gave a little affection back to her.

She had no illusions as to the reason Paul remained, publicly anyway, at her side. She had no children, no heirs and she was very, very generous to him. Apart from the enormous allowance she gave him, she was always buying him extravagant presents. In return, Paul observed most of the rules of the game. He was always affectionate to her in public; played the part of the devoted lover even when he was having an affair with another woman. He kept his infidelities discreetly in the background and would have pretended they had never happened had she wished it. But after an affair was over, she would derive some comfort from hearing about it from a disenchanted Paul, who would always compare the girl he had tired of unfavourably with Yvonne.

'I must have been mad, *chérie,*' he would say. 'I can't think what possessed me to hurt you so cruelly for a few moments' pleasure with a woman like that. Forgive me, *chérie*. You know I love you.'

And she could pretend until the next time, to herself and to him, that she did believe him, that all was forgiven and forgotten.

He had long ago given up his ambition to become an actor and was now Yvonne's manager. Her parents had died leaving her their château and a large estate in Normandy and Paul dealt with the accounts and various problems that arose with tenant farmers and leases and such like. He did so efficiently and the investments he made for Yvonne on the stock market were equally shrewd and successful. The allowance Yvonne gave him he could justifiably be said to have earned and the arrangement suited them both perfectly.

Once, when he had been asking her to sign some documents that required her signature urgently, she had said, half teasing but half seriously:

'If we were married, Paul, *you* could sign all these tiresome papers and we should both be much happier.'

To her dismay, Paul had acted completely out of character, turning a dull red
and even stuttering a little as he replied:

'No, Yvonne, I will not be tied!'

Hurt as well as surprised, she had tried
to laugh off the moment.

'I was only joking, *chéri!* Of course I
don't wish to tie you. But if there is one
thing I hate, it is signing dull old papers
like these.'

There had been only one other occasion
when marriage had been mentioned between them. It was after the end of one
of Paul's affairs. He had held her in his
arms, wiped the tears from her cheeks and
said remorsefully:

'It was unforgivable of me to hurt you
so, my darling. What can I do to earn your
forgiveness? To make you happy again?'

She had tried to explain to him that her
greatest unhappiness came, not from the
act of infidelity itself which she could bring
herself to overlook since it meant so little
to him, but her own feelings of insecurity
whilst a new affair was in progress.

'I can never be *sure*, Paul, that it will
come to an end.'

'But, my love, I always come back to
you, you know that. I have only to be

a short while in the company of another woman to realise how, very, very much you mean to me.'

'But, Paul, one day you might find someone else. You might be tempted to leave me. How can I *know* for sure? It would be different if we were married; if you were my husband. Paul...'

'I have never pretended to you, Yvonne. I won't marry you. *I won't be tied.* If it is marriage you want, I shall have to leave you.'

This time, needing to understand, she had asked for an explanation.

'What is so dreadful about marriage?' she persisted. 'It would make no difference to our way of life.'

But he had refused to explain.

'I won't be tied!' he said again, coldly, factually and finally.

So, as she had learned to accept other things from Paul, she had had to accept this, too. It would have been easier if she had understood why he was so much against marriage. He must know she would not tie him in the way he seemed to fear; that she would continue to turn a blind eye when he wanted a week or two with some other woman. Financially he stood to gain a fortune. She could not follow his reasoning and sometimes wondered if it had its roots in some episode in his childhood. Perhaps his father and mother were unhappily married. He would not talk about his childhood or the days prior to his meeting her so she could only guess—and hope that one day Paul would change his mind.

'You are not to worry about me, Monika. I count myself as a fortunate woman, despite what you may think to the contrary. In his way Paul loves me, and I love him. It is not every woman who can say as much. I count my blessings! Now, Monika, what do you say to a cup of lemon tea?'

It was Yvonne's way of saying that the subject of Paul was closed for the time being. Monika accepted her wish and, filled with uneasy sympathy for her friend, proceeded to talk about the less important issues in a woman's life—hair and clothes.

They lay back in their chairs and the intense heat of the afternoon sun slowly dried Yvonne's lashes where they had been wetted by her unshed tears.

8

It was some time before Paul could attract Ann's attention from the skiers. She was fascinated and a little shocked to find how good they were. Up at these heights, there was a very different standard than she was used to admiring on the nursery slopes.

'I'll never be able to do that!' she said. Or: 'I wish I could weave from side to side the way that woman is doing.'

Perhaps the most depressing but intriguing sight of all were the four- to five-year-olds, every bit as much at home on these slopes as the tots who raced past her down below.

But at last Paul managed to bring her thoughts back to himself.

'Are you glad you came up here with me?' he asked her.

She looked back at him, eyes shining.

'Oh, yes! It's all so different. It's hard to believe only two weeks ago I was in dreary old England!'

He smiled back at her.

'I, too, am glad you came to Aiguille. Tell me, Ann, had you no regrets leaving your home?'

'Regrets?' Ann asked surprised. 'But why should I? It's only for a year and this is the most fabulous experience for me.'

'Then there is no one in particular you care about in England? No one you minded leaving behind?'

'Oh!' Ann's eyes dropped as she understood Paul's question. 'A boy friend, you mean. No, no one special.'

'That is good!' Paul said. 'Tell me, Ann, have you ever been in love?'

For a moment she was childishly tempted to boast a little—to invent a few really serious love affairs. But her natural honesty forbade it.

'No!' she answered truthfully. 'Once or twice I thought I was, but it was just wishful thinking or momentary attention or something.'

Paul leant back in his chair, his face unexpectedly serious.

'I don't suppose you will believe this,' he said, 'but I have never been "in love" either.'

Ann's face broke into a smile.

'What nonsense!' she laughed. 'You

150

don't really think I'll take that seriously, do you?'

'No!' agreed Paul, still unsmiling. 'I am aware that it sounds ridiculous. Nonetheless, it is quite true. I have never met anyone for whom I cared more about than I care about myself.'

Ann looked at him thoughtfully. It was impossible not to take him seriously now. He sounded perfectly genuine.

'That isn't a very nice thing to say about yourself,' she said gently. 'Anyway, I'm sure it isn't really true.'

He leant forward on his elbows and stared directly into Ann's eyes.

'If we are to be friends, Ann, it is best you know the truth about me. I am not really a very nice person. A lot of what people will tell you about me is true. I do not much like myself.'

Ann was at loss to reply. It seemed out of character for Paul Duret to be talking in this self-disparaging fashion.

'I don't listen to gossip,' she said finally. 'So you don't have to worry about what other people say. I make my own friends where and how I please!'

'Ah, a brave declaration!' Paul said softly. 'I hope very much that it is true.

Tell me, then, if you would have me for your friend no matter what you heard to my discredit?'

'Well, yes!' Ann said hesitantly. 'Of course I would if I liked you.'

'And do you?'

There was no avoiding a reply. She decided once more upon honesty.

'I don't really know you!' she admitted. 'I think I do.'

She was well aware that physical attraction and liking were two separate emotions. The first certainly existed as far as Paul was concerned but whether or not she liked him as a person she could not yet be certain.

'You don't think the difference in our ages could be a barrier to our friendship?'

'I suppose it could,' she agreed. 'I realise I may seem rather childish and young to you and I'd quite understand if you found my company boring.'

'I don't find you dull at all, Ann, but perhaps you find me so?'

'Why ever should I?' Ann argued surprised. 'I mean, older people have much more to talk about and they've done things and seen things and...well, I'm probably not explaining myself very well but personally I like the company of people older than myself!'

As if it were the most natural thing in the world, Paul took and held Ann's hand in his.

'Would you permit me to tell you a little about Madame Verdos?' he said quickly.

'Madame Verdos?' Ann felt suddenly anxious to drop this conversation. Without knowing why, she did not wish to hear whatever he was about to say. 'Please don't tell me anything you'd rather not. I mean...'

'I want you to understand my relationship with her,' Paul broke in. 'If we are to be friends, you and I, it is best that you should know the situation.'

Ann felt out of her depth. He ignored her discomfort and went on:

'I met her many years ago when I was a very young man. She was extremely nice to me, and kind; helped me to make my way in the world. I am, therefore, permanently obligated to her. You understand this?'

'I think so!' Ann said uncertainly.

'I am not tied to her in any way except through my gratitude for what she has done for me,' Paul said in a strangely harsh voice. 'I have told her that I will never marry her and she has no doubts as to this. Nevertheless, she is very fond of me and it is obligatory for me to be as kind and attentive to her as I can. I manage her business affairs and I live in her house as one of the family. Many people disapprove of this arrangement on the grounds of convention but she needs someone to look after her and protect her. I am, of course, perfectly free to come and go as I choose. Do you understand, Ann?'

It was as near the truth as he dared go. He was not, however, prepared for Ann's bluntness.

'You mean, you live with her but you are not actually having an affair with her?'

To many women Paul had replied to such a question negatively. For some reason, the customary lie would not come out spontaneously to Ann. Whilst he hesitated, she said:

'I may be very young, Paul, but I wasn't born yesterday. It is none of my business in any case. We can still be friends even if...'

'Ann, I am not in love with her. I don't love her. What I have done in the past is out of necessity, gratitude—call it what you will. It is important to me that you should understand. If...if it makes any difference between us, I will break with Yvonne completely.'

He had not known beforehand that he was going to make such a declaration. He was not even sure if he could carry out such an intention. He only knew that for this moment in time, anyway, he really meant it.

Ann was confused. She could no longer be in any doubt that Paul Duret was seriously interested in her. Until this afternoon, she had been far from sure that he meant anything more than to have the mildest flirtation with her. Now, suddenly, he was saying that for her sake, he would end his affair with the French woman if she, Ann, wished it.

She was flattered, relieved, excited and at the same time, deeply disturbed. She felt totally out of her depth for she had never really allowed herself to think seriously about Paul. What *did* he mean to her? Could she fall in love with him? Was she already a little in love with him?

'Ann, please do not look so worried!' he was saying. 'I did not wish to upset you. It is just that my emotions overcame me.

You have this strange effect upon me that makes me feel first and think afterwards. I am very much afraid that I am falling in love with you.'

Now the word was out in the open, lying between them like a tangible object. Afraid of it, Ann said defensively:

'That's absurd. We hardly know each other!'

'Is that not how love is? Sudden? Swift?'

'Not always!' Ann argued. 'This could be nothing but mutual attraction.'

'Mutual?' Paul said quickly. 'Then you feel it, too, Ann? There *is* something between us. It has been there every time we danced; every time you looked at me and I at you; every time we have been near each other.'

Ann knew it was true. There had been this strange magnetism, drawing her eyes to where he stood at the bar; making her conscious of herself and him when they were in the same room—a continual awareness of him as a man.

'I don't think we should be talking like this,' she said with an attempt to bring the conversation back to normal. 'It's much, much too soon for us to know how we really feel about each other. Anyway, I...I

156

don't even know what love is. Please, Paul, let's not be so serious. Can't we just have fun together? Be friends? Be happy?'

Paul gave the barest shrug of his shoulders.

'I don't know!' he said. 'We will try if that is what you want. I want only what you want, Ann.'

Quite suddenly, he remembered Yvonne speaking those self-same words to him. 'I want only what you want, Paul!' The memory made him ashamed—an emotion he had never before experienced. Because Yvonne was the cause of his discomfort, he felt suddenly angry with her.

'She shall not come between Ann and me,' he thought with acute violence.

He turned his head to look at the girl beside him. Her eyes were on the skiers once more but he guessed by the tell-tale colour in her cheeks that she was, in fact, thinking about him. The violence within him gave way to a rush of tenderness. She was so very young, so totally innocent and untouched by life. Had he the right to reach out for that innocence and turn it into knowledge? He was almost afraid to touch her and yet knew that given the chance, he would not hesitate. He wanted her as he had never wanted any woman before. It was more than just physical desire. He needed her for reasons he did not even know himself; for that very quality of youth and innocence that never had been and never could be his.

Ann's thoughts were not about him but about Yvonne Verdos. She was trying hard to view Paul's story with adult eyes. He had said he didn't love her yet he had been having an affair with her. Somehow the thought was violently objectionable to her, Ann. If Paul had been in love with the older woman, she would not have felt so badly about the relationship.

Yet, she argued with herself, if his motives were to prove his gratitude to the woman who had helped him, was it so wrong? He had said Yvonne Verdos loved him but that he had told her honestly he would never marry her. Was it so wrong then, for him to give her affection, company, understanding, sympathy—everything, in fact, but love and marriage?

She tried not to ask herself if he were still making love to her. It was not her business and yet the idea appalled her. She remembered Paul's declaration that he would terminate his relationship with Yvonne Verdos if she, Ann, wished it. She did wish it. She wished even more that such an arrangement did not exist to be terminated.

Suddenly, she realised what it was Luc had tried to warn her about. No doubt he knew of Paul's affair with the older woman. Out of respect for Ann's innocence, he had not liked to come out with the bare facts. Well, she could put his mind at rest—she knew the worst now! In one way, the fact that Paul had a mistress was objectionable to her and yet, in another, it was strangely exciting. It made Paul a little 'dangerous' and so very different from the boys at home. It was as if, through being friends with him herself, she had entered into a new, sophisticated, worldly society far removed from the teenage strata of home and family.

'You are making up your mind whether you should put me out of your life?' Paul broke into her thoughts with an astuteness she found unnerving. 'I beg you not to judge me harshly, Ann. You must remember that no matter how it may look to you, I had only the kindest motives towards Yvonne. Other people, who do not know the facts, may consider I have "used" her, but I assure you, I have only acted from my feelings of indebtedness.'

Ann felt embarrassed. She did not feel old enough or grown-up enough to 'judge' Paul at all, yet he was talking to her as an equal and somehow, she must strive to behave like one. At the same time, she was simply not sure what to reply. She was not in any way sure how she felt about Paul in relation to herself, let alone in relation to anyone else.

'Aren't we getting far too serious?' she prevaricated. 'I mean, I don't honestly think you have any need to explain your behaviour to me. I appreciate you wanting to be honest with me and in a way, I'm glad you did tell me everything, but...well, let's not talk about it any more. Please?'

Paul knew better than to push her. She was not yet ready for a declaration of love from him. Perhaps he had been too precipitate talking so frankly and yet he had no alternative if he wished to put his side of the case before Luc Menton did. He hoped he hadn't frightened her off. He had forgotten how romantic and idealistic a young girl of Ann's age could be.

'You are right!' he said with an assumed

lightness of tone. 'We are being far too serious—especially on such a lovely day. Please forget what I said, Ann. I would not have been so frank but for the fact that I value your good opinion. Now, let me order you some lemon tea. It would be very refreshing, no?'

Before long, Ann felt quite at ease again and began really to enjoy the afternoon. Paul was gay, amusing and attentive. Sometimes he would hold her hand as if it were a perfectly ordinary and natural thing to do and she tried to behave as if the physical contact meant nothing to her, either. In fact, each time he touched her, even if it were only lightly on the shoulder or elbow, she felt a quick thrill of excitement course through her body. She had never before been so conscious of anyone's proximity or of her own trembling reactions.

It never crossed her mind that Paul's gestures were premeditated and calculated to bring just such a reaction. His manner was casual and he himself appeared unconscious of the contact. In fact, he was watching her slow awakening to desire with delight. He noted, without appearing to do so, the heightening colour in her cheeks, the quick fluttering of her eyelashes and the ill-concealed trembling of her hand beneath his. This pleasure had in it both cruelty, since it was deliberately evoked, and tenderness—an emotion so foreign to him that this, too, gave him pleasure.

But Paul had been too long a self-centred, selfish and inconsiderate man, ever ready to exploit any woman to achieve his own satisfaction. Now he could not desist from drawing this young girl further and further into the net he had devised for her seduction. The dawning love he felt for her was very much in abeyance to the growing desire to possess her. It never once crossed his mind that if he really cared about her, the kindest thing he could do would be to leave her alone and not involve her with a worthless, jaded character like himself. Ann's first experience of love should have been with a young, decent thinking, romantic boy like Luc Menton. Paul knew it yet never gave it a serious moment of consideration. His own desires came very much first and Ann's happiness was only of secondary consideration.

To Yvonne Verdos's feelings, he gave no thought at all.

9

'I am very sorry, Ann, but I do not feel it would be right for me to permit it!'

Ann looked at Madame Menton's face, for once not smiling but anxious and distressed. She was astonished by this reply to her announcement that she would be dining that evening with Paul Duret. She had expected opposition from Luc but it had never occurred to her that Madame might intervene in such a manner in her arrangements.

'But, Madame, for what reason do you object?'

They were speaking in French and Ann had difficulty in finding the necessary vocabulary.

'He is not a correct companion for you. I am certain your Mama would not wish me to permit it!' Madame Menton repeated firmly.

'Not correct? You mean, because he is older?' Ann asked.

163

'No, that is not what I mean!' Madame answered slowly.

Ann's cheeks burned. All the way down in the cable car from the Point, she had felt uneasy about accepting Paul's invitation to dine. She wanted to accept but she dreaded having to tell Luc. That she had told Madame was a mere formality—a courtesy she felt due to her hostess. It had not once occurred to her that Madame would raise objections; nor that Paul would come under discussion in this fashion.

'You mean, because of his association with Madame Verdos?' she said as bravely as she could.

It was Madame Menton's turn to look uncomfortable.

'You are a well-brought-up young girl, Ann. I do not think it would be right for you to be seen out with a man with Monsieur Duret's reputation.'

'But I'm not a schoolgirl!' Ann protested hotly. 'I am quite old enough to take care of myself.'

'I do not question your motives, Ann!' Madame Menton replied patiently. 'But I question the motives Monsieur Duret may have.'

'Really, Madame!' Ann cried, the more

164

vehemently because she herself was uncertain whether her own mother would have taken Madame's view had she been here. 'I really don't see what harm could come to me over a dinner date. I can take care of myself. Besides, I think it's very unfair to attribute any ulterior motives to Paul. He just wants to be friends!'

'What! That gigolo!' Luc, his voice, filled with sarcasm, spoke from the recess of the armchair where he had been buried behind a book.

Ann swung round to face him, her temper rising.

'I don't see what this has got to do with you,' she flared. 'And Paul isn't a gigolo. You're just saying the first nasty word that comes to mind because you're jealous!'

The instant she spoke them, she wished the words back. They were unfair and the look on Luc's face, now white and taut, showed her only too clearly that her barb had struck home.

'I'm sorry, Luc!' she said. 'I didn't mean...'

But before she could end her apology, Luc had risen to his feet and walked out of the room.

Ann felt like bursting into tears. If she

had known Paul's invitation was going to create such a scene, she would have refused it. But it had seemed harmless enough and she wanted to go...to complete what had been a wonderful and exciting afternoon in his company.

She looked with distress at Luc's mother. 'Honestly, I didn't mean to upset him!' she said truthfully. 'It just struck me as so unfair that he should say such things about Paul when they are quite untrue. It's a horrible thing to say about any man, especially when he isn't there to defend himself.'

'Monsieur Duret seems to have found an excellent advocate in you,' Madame Menton said gently but shrewdly. 'As to Luc, I am very much afraid your accusation was fair. He *is* jealous. He is very fond of you, Ann. He wishes, like me, to protect you.'

Ann sighed.

'I know, Madame. I appreciate the fact that you and Luc are thinking of my good, but I just can't see what harm there is in eating a meal and dancing with Paul Duret. We'll be at the club with dozens of other people around. I'll have plenty of chaperones!'

166

Her attempt to lighten the tone of the discussion did not succeed. Madame replied:

'It is your reputation at stake, Ann. If you are seen with Paul Duret, everyone will draw the conclusion, rightly or wrongly, that you are his girl.'

'Well, what about all the evenings I've spent with Luc at the club?' Ann countered.

'That is very different,' Madame said sharply. 'Luc does not himself have a reputation for the seduction of young ladies. Therefore nothing will have been assumed from your association with him but that he enjoys your company and that you enjoy his. With Monsieur Duret, it will be otherwise, I assure you.'

'I am beginning to see now why Paul warned me people in Aiguille would speak against him!' Ann said unhappily. 'Just because he is attractive to women, the men dislike him and...'

'Ann, people are not so stupid as you might wish to believe. Men like Paul Duret do not come by such reputations because of one or two minor indiscretions. He is well known in Aiguille and what is known about him is not good. Please believe that

I do not say such things lightly. I am not in any way prejudiced, but I must warn you that Luc spoke only the truth.'

'Well, I just don't believe it. I happen to *know* the truth about Paul's affair with Madame Verdos. That's what you are referring to, isn't it? Paul told me all about it and I think it is very unfair that he should be accused of being a gigolo just because she once helped him up in the world and he is grateful to her. That's a very different thing from being kept by a woman, isn't it?'

Madame Menton was silent. She was secretly shocked to hear that Ann's friendship with Duret had developed so far that he had actually referred to his affair with Madam Verdos to her. In her circle, people did not speak of such matters to young girls, not even to their daughters. She felt outraged and confused at the same time. She was quite certain in her own mind that Ann's mother would not countenance such a friendship, even though she knew that in England parental authority was much more permissive these days than it had been a few years ago. Nevertheless, she had to find some way to prevent Ann from associating with such a profligate and that Paul Duret was a profligate she was in no doubt.

'I do have a responsibility towards you—to your parents,' she said at last. 'I cannot forbid you to see this man but I do request that you should not go out with him unless your mother first gives her permission. I hope you will not think it unreasonable of me so to direct a visitor in my home, but I, like Luc, have become very fond of you, Ann. You have become much like a daughter to me and I would be most unhappy if you would not agree to wait at least until your mother has written her approval.'

It was Ann's turn to remain silent. She had never anticipated such a situation. Madame could not actually control her movements but as a guest, Ann did not feel she had the right deliberately to flout her wishes, especially when she had put her side of the picture fairly and reasonably.

'I will write to my mother tonight,' she said, 'if that will make you happier, Madame. But I am sure she trusts me enough to let me make my own friends and to judge for myself what is good or bad. I promise you I will tell her all about Paul.'

'And you will telephone Monsieur Duret and cancel your date for this evening?'

'If you insist!' Ann agreed.

Madame thanked her warmly for easing her mind and Ann went to her own room, deeply depressed. Not only was there the anti-climax to the day now that she would not, after all, be seeing Paul, but there was her own uneasy feeling that her mother might side with Madame.

'It really is too silly!' Ann told herself. 'I'm nearly nineteen. I should be able to choose my own friends at my age!'

And in the last resort, she knew that she could flout both her mother's and Madame's wishes and see Paul as often as she pleased. But she did not want that. She wanted their approval. She wanted them to like him as much as she did. He may have got himself a bad reputation but that didn't mean he was bad. If he'd been the kind of man the Mentons suggested, he wouldn't have been honest enough to tell her the truth about himself. He would have denied anything deprecatory to himself. As to his being a gigolo—that, too, was ridiculous. Madame Verdos employed him as her manager. Naturally she paid him a salary.

She sat down at her desk to write to her mother but the sentences would not come easily. The facts about Paul did not look good on paper and when she sought to explain them, it looked as if she were trying to excuse or whitewash him.

She tore up several attempts before, finally, she wrote a version she felt fair to both herself and Paul.

...I think his past flirtations have been grossly exaggerated and you know how proper the Swiss are! Madame is very nice and means well, but she's still living in the Victorian era when chaperones were required for girls of my age. I expect you and Dad will laugh at the idea of my having to request permission to go out with a man but there it is—Madame won't be happy till you give me your okay.

It seems particularly silly when Paul is just a friend. Anyone would think I was in love with him or likely to be. Actually, I see twenty times more of Luc but of course, Madame does not worry about him as he is her son.

So be a dear and drop Madame a line, will you, letting her know I'm quite old and sane enough to go out with anyone I want and there is no need for her to vet my boy friends!

The remainder of the letter spoke only of the magnificence of the view from the Point and how happy and content she was with the life out here.

The letter written Ann went downstairs to the hall to telephone Paul. She was not looking forward to the conversation and had put off the moment in cowardly fashion, for which she now secretly reproved herself. It was going to be so awkward explaining the reasons for breaking the date.

As she requested the telephone operator to give her Madame Verdos's number, Ann felt another moment of uneasiness. Supposing Madame and not Paul or the maid were to answer? What would she say?

But fortunately she was saved any such embarrassment. Paul himself answered the telephone. He sounded more than a little surprised when she told him who was speaking and his reply was curt and without warmth when she explained the reason for her call.

'Naturally I am very disappointed!' he said coldly. 'I presume there is a good reason?'

'No, it's a silly reason!' Ann replied dejectedly. 'I can't really explain now, Paul, but I will next time I see you. Please believe me, I am as disappointed as you are.'

'You will not alter your mind?'

'I *can't!*' Ann told him. 'But I hope it is just a question of postponement, Paul. Next week, I should be able to make it if you want.'

'Next week!' he repeated. 'But...' He broke off suddenly as if he had changed his mind about arguing with her. 'Very well, it is as you wish, naturally,' he said, again using that cold, distant tone of voice. *'Au revoir!'*

Ann could not know and certainly did not imagine that Paul's end of the conversation had been severely restricted by the fact that Yvonne Verdos was in the adjoining room and might overhear what he had to say. She guessed only that he was disappointed and angry and no doubt thought her unreasonable and capricious, to go back so quickly on the promise made earlier in the afternoon. Paul had foreseen that the Mentons might raise objections and when he'd mentioned the fact to her, she had replied:

'They can't stop me going out with you if I want, Paul! Of course I'll come.'

Now here she was, prevented from meeting him, as good as forbidden to do so. Sitting in the cable car, her hand clasped tightly in his, it had seemed so easy to be brave about standing up to the Mentons' objections, but when it came to the point, she had been weak and childish. She had prepared herself for Luc's disapproval but not for his mother's.

As she turned to go back to her room, her face clearly indicating her depression, Luc came down the stairs blocking her way.

'Ann, I want to apologise. I had no right to interfere in your conversation with Maman.'

She was taken off guard by the gentle apology, knowing that if an apology were due at all, it was not from Luc but from her. Pride would not let her make it. She said stiffly:

'Forget it. You'll be pleased to hear I've cancelled my date.'

The look of relief on Luc's face annoyed her further. She didn't want to believe that he was genuinely worried about her. She had enough to think about without being troubled over Luc's feelings. She felt doubly guilty remembering her afternoon, on the Point. Had Luc guessed by now she had spent the time with Paul? He must know she'd seen Paul in order for them to have made a date for the evening.

This awareness of Luc's concern with her movements added to her irritation. It was time he understood that she meant to come and go as she pleased without being answerable to him. His proprietary manner towards her was quite unjustified. Madame Menton did at least have the excuse of acting in place of her own mother but Luc could hardly claim the rights of an older brother.

Even as the thought flashed through her mind, Ann knew she was not being fair. She had been perfectly prepared to accept all Luc's many kindnesses and attentions whilst she wanted them. She was being unreasonable to reject his interest in her now just because it no longer suited her.

'Look, Luc, I'm the one who owes you an apology!' she said impulsively, her face softening as her mood changed. 'I was angry because I felt you and your mother were both being so unfair to Paul Duret. I honestly don't believe he is as bad as both of you think and since we have agreed to be friends, I can't sit back and hear him condemned so totally without sticking up for him. Surely that is the least one friend can do for another?'

Luc led the way into the sittingroom, his expression one of uneasiness.

'Friends? You and Paul Duret?' he echoed. 'But why, Ann? Why *him?*'

'Why not?' Ann countered. 'I know *you* don't like him, Luc, but I do. And he likes me. Haven't I the right to make my own friends?'

'Yes, of course!' Luc answered stiffly. 'Please forgive me for interfering. Had it been any other man but Duret, I would have minded my own business. I had to speak out about him. He is not to be trusted, Ann, and since you are a stranger in my country I felt it my duty to warn you about him.'

'Okay, so you've warned me!' Ann said with an attempt at flippancy. 'I am now well aware of Paul's evil reputation, his past affairs and the probability that he wants to seduce me. So forewarned, I'm perfectly safe in his company, aren't I?'

Luc did not reply. There were times when Ann sounded so very young, he wanted to put her over his knee and spank her. But more than anything in the world, he wanted to protect her. He was very much afraid he was going to be powerless to do so.

'If it had been any other man...' he thought again, yet deep down inside him, he questioned the honesty of such a thought. No matter how acceptable and nice another man might be, could he stand back and watch Ann falling in love?

He knew the answer only too well. Her accusation had been nearer the mark than she might have realised. He *was* desperately jealous. Moreover, he was deeply and hopelessly in love with Ann and he wanted her for himself. It was all as simple as that.

'You and I are still friends, are we not?' he asked with all the restraint he could muster.

Ann turned to him with one of her quick, impulsive movements, her face relaxed and smiling.

'But *of course*, we are!' she cried. 'It's so silly for us to be quarrelling like this. It isn't as if Paul was all that important. It's really more a matter of principle. I just want to be able to choose my own friends.

I should have been just as adamant about wanting to go on knowing you if someone else had tried to stop me seeing you.' She gave a schoolgirl giggle. 'Not that you have poor Paul's terrible reputation!'

Luc smiled.

'It really is no laughing matter all the same,' he persisted. 'It will reflect on you, Ann, no matter how innocent your intentions. This is why Maman and I are so worried!'

'I know!' Ann agreed. 'I'm honestly not being stubborn, Luc, but it seems so unfair. Even if you are right and he had been a profligate in the past, it doesn't mean he will go on behaving badly all his life, does it? Maybe he has reached the age where he's grown tired of all the flirtations and affairs and wants to take life more seriously. How can he if everywhere he goes he's never allowed to mix with decent people?'

Luc frowned.

'I had not realised you were a reformer, Ann.'

Ann coloured slightly.

'Well, I'm not—at least, I've never yet tried to reform anyone. I don't even know if Paul Duret *needs* reforming. You've almost got *me* believing he's a black sheep now!'

It crossed Luc's mind that he was going quite the wrong way about putting Ann off Duret. The more he blackened him, the greater seemed Ann's desire to champion him. It could well be that between them, he and his mother had precipitated just the very effect they had been seeking to avoid.

'Well, I've said my last word about Paul Duret!' he told her. 'What is much more important to me, Ann, is that our friendship should not be disturbed by all this.'

'Oh, Luc, of course not!' Ann cried sincerely. 'I'm so glad you said that. I knew you disliked Paul and I was anxious how you would feel about me seeing him. Now you know and accept that I mean to go on being friends with him, it makes everything all right again between you and me. I was miserable all afternoon knowing I'd really deceived you. Honestly, Luc, I wanted to tell you I was going up to the Point with Paul but I couldn't.'

With a tremendous effort, Luc hid his sense of shock. He had had no idea until this moment that she had spent the afternoon in Duret's company. He had assumed she'd run into him in the village. Now he was beginning better to understand how she had become so much more deeply involved with Paul Duret. He had had a whole afternoon in which to brain-wash her.

His dislike of the older man intensified. For the first time in his life, Luc felt almost murderous. If Duret were to harm one hair of Ann's head, he would kill him! he thought. But he was learning fast and he hid his reactions from Ann, appearing quite unconcerned by her announcement.

'It is very beautiful up at the Point, is it not?' he asked her casually. 'It must have been lovely there on the terrace.'

Now it was Ann's turn to hide her reactions. She had expected Luc at the very least to frown and tell her she should not have gone there with Paul; to reprove her for having lied about her afternoon activities.

They discussed the scenery for a moment or two and then Luc said:

'Since you have broken your date for tonight, Ann, perhaps you would allow me to take you to the cinema? There is a very good film I think you might enjoy.

180

Of course, it will be in French but I think you will easily follow it. It is very rare that we have good films up here so it would be a pity to miss it.'

Ann hesitated. She would like to go but suppose Paul saw her there with Luc? He'd be terribly hurt, believing she had cut their date in order to go with Luc to the cinema.

'Please come, Ann. If you say no, I shall think you are still annoyed with me!' Luc urged gently.

Ann smiled.

'Okay, I'd love to!' she said quite truthfully. It wouldn't be the same as the evening with Paul but at least it would be something to do to stop her moping at having to break her date. And if it would help to put things right between her and Luc, she was quite happy to go with him. The very last thing she wanted to do was to be at odds with Luc. She was really fond of him and he'd been so good to her.

They did not run into Paul on the short walk to the cinema at the far end of the village. Ann was relieved and forgot her problems as she sat back to enjoy the musical with Luc. Halfway through the

181

programme the couple in front put their arms around each other and occasionally stopped watching the film to kiss. Ann, observing them, knew that Luc must have seen them, too, and wondered if he would try to hold her hand and how she would feel if he tried to kiss her on the way home.

But Luc seemed immersed in the film and only turned his head occasionally towards her to enquire if she understood the dialogue.

During the walk home, he held her arm to steady her on the hard-packed snow but although his voice and words were warm and friendly, he made no further move to indicate that she meant more to him than the most casual of friends. She thought of the evening when he had practically confessed he was falling in love with her; of the way he kissed her then. If she really did mean anything to him, he had found a strange way of showing it this evening. To anyone seeing them together, they would appear only the most casual of acquaintances!

In one way Ann was relieved. She was not sure how she would have coped with Luc in an amorous mood. Yet perversely, she was piqued and a little worried that he had changed his mind about her after her behaviour today. If he had changed towards her, she could hardly blame him. He must dislike her very much for the way she had lied to him about the afternoon; the way she had accused him in front of his mother of acting out of jealousy. In all, she had not behaved in the least admirably and it would be small wonder if Luc had decided she wasn't after all worth caring about deeply.

As they reached the house, Ann's enjoyment of the film was totally forgotten in a wave of depression. Luc did not suggest a late-night cup of coffee and perhaps a chat in front of the dying fire as he had the other evening. He bade her a courteous goodnight and left her no alternative but to go straight up to bed.

She lay awake for some time, pondering on the strangeness of people's moods. Her own moods varied from hour to hour so she should not be surprised if other people's did, too. Yet she had thought of Luc as someone completely dependable. Now she wasn't sure about him any more. She wasn't even certain he would want to take her for her usual ski-ing lesson in the morning for he had said nothing about it as was his custom last thing at night.

Perhaps it was as well, she thought sleepily. Paul would probably be watching out for her and she particularly wished to see Paul alone so that she could explain that she had not broken their date of her own choice. She hoped very much that Paul would not think the situation so childish he wished nothing more to do with her. The simplest way would be to explain that Madame Menton would not permit her to go out with anyone other than Luc without her mother's permission and whilst she, herself, thought this absurd, she had to conform to Madame Menton's wishes until her mother's reply came stating she could accept any invitations she wished.

Thoughts of Paul and the way he had held her hand, looked at her, spoken to her, filled her mind. Almost asleep, it occurred to her that she was not really a very nice person, wanting Luc to stay a little in love with her when she, herself, was already a little in love with another man.

'It's high time I grew up!' she told herself and at once fell into a child's deep, instant and untroubled sleep.

10

Paul did not need to be told the reason for Ann's last-minute phone call. He guessed that the Mentons had forbidden her to see him. He was furiously angry yet powerless to do anything until the morning.

Yvonne had been in the adjoining room when Ann phoned. If she overheard his side of the conversation, she had not asked any questions or even who had been on the telephone. Returning to the salon, he had said:

'I shan't be going out this evening, Yvonne. If you would like to go to the club later, I will be free to escort you if you wish.'

Yvonne eyed his face thoughtfully. She knew his every expression. She could see by the drawn brows, the sulky droop of his mouth that this new affair was not going so well. He had returned from his afternoon in the gayest of spirits and her heart had sunk into a dull dejection, believing that all had gone as he wished with his new

185

girl. Now, hope was raised once again. But she would not question him. He would, of course, lie if she tried to force the truth from him so it was better for both of them if she kept her feelings to herself. Long experience had shown her that her wisest course was to ride out these episodes in assumed ignorance. She would never force a showdown. To do so might mean losing Paul altogether.

'I am a little tired. Too much sun, perhaps. I was sunbathing all the afternoon on the terrace with Monika. Perhaps I shall feel better after supper!'

She did not wish to go to the club with Paul. He would only join a group of men at the bar and leave her to talk to some woman friend whilst she tried not to watch him flirting with some pretty woman on a stool near him. There was no enjoyment for her in such an evening, when Paul's mind was elsewhere. At least when they stayed at home, she had all his attention.

But this was not strictly true, she told herself, as she watched Paul pour himself another drink and pace the floor restlessly. He picked up a paper, glanced through it, put it down and lit a cigarette. He walked to the window and back and sat down only

186

to stand up again a moment or two later. He was like a restless, caged lion and she knew she could not spend an evening with him in one of these moods. She would have to go out with him—or send him out alone.

'I am too old for him!' she thought as she sipped a Dubonnet and tried not to look at him. 'If I were younger, I could go out on a mad binge, get drunk, come home and let him make love to me!'

But she didn't want this. She never drank heavily and now, if she had even a little too much, it upset her digestion and prevented her sleeping properly. Moreover, she had a headache and did not feel young or gay. But she knew she must make the effort. Paul was so quickly bored. If she let herself relax, vegetate a little, he would become petulant and demanding like a small boy whose mother will not take him out to play.

'I am old and he is so very, very young!' she thought. 'Won't he ever grow up? Mature? Catch up with me so that we can settle down and grow old together?'

She knew the answer. It was not in Paul to be a husband. Some inner insecurity in his make-up—perhaps because of his childhood—demanded a continual succession of conquests. He needed constant flattery. It wasn't enough that *she* loved him, needed him, flattered him. He had always to have a circle of feminine admirers, himself in the centre, gay, amusing, the life and soul of the party. If there were no one to watch and admire, he was unable to sustain his gay frivolity and became morose and dejected.

'Poor Paul!' she thought. It was strange, this new ability to feel sorry for him. Far more often, she was feeling sorry for herself. Now there were times when she even saw her love for a man like Paul as faintly ridiculous. There was so little about him that was worth the kind of love she had to give. Even if he wished, he could not return such a love for it was not in him to live on the intellectual level which was naturally hers. She had always had to bring herself down to Paul's level. He could never meet her on her own.

And Paul's level was really very basic. He was the perfect lover in a purely physical sense. He was a woman's man. He understood women's moods, needs, desires. He had perfected his part in the ritual of love-making. His technique might have been thought by some women to be the result of acute sensitivity; to a real awareness of what went on inside a woman's heart. But Yvonne knew this was not so. Paul had merely studied women as other men studied their hobbies. He provided what they wanted because it meant he could achieve his own will by doing so. Any woman he made love to fell a little in love with him. Yvonne could understand it. His timing was perfect and he never forgot the all-important details like the tender kiss that followed after love-making; the little unexpected gifts; the compliments; the way in which he could make make a woman believe she was the only one in the world who mattered to him. And all of it, Yvonne knew, was simply part of his technique.

Perhaps the bitterest pill of all to swallow, when she knew Paul was making love to some other woman, was the knowledge that there had been a time when Paul had had nothing but his looks and his charm to endear him to the opposite sex. She had taught him everything he knew. He had been an apt pupil. He never forgot and her greatest torment lay in imagining Paul loving other women as she had shown him how to make love to her.

Such occasions were comparatively rare now. At the end of an affair, Paul would return rather like a guilty schoolboy wanting forgiveness. But he had to tell her all about it first and then, when she begged him to stop thinking, talking about it and forget, as she intended to do, that such a woman had ever existed, he would reward her forgiveness by making love to her. She knew very well that he did not do so from genuine desire and she had to fight with her pride in order to meet Paul on such terms. She forced herself not to think about the other woman from whose arms he had so recently come back to her. She closed her eyes and pretended that Paul's whispered words were the real truth—'I've only ever really loved you, *chérie!*'

They dined and went to the club. As Yvonne had anticipated, Paul soon left her to join some friends at the bar. She noticed that he was not really participating in their conversation. His eyes were searching the room continually; watching the door. She knew then that he was looking for the English girl. She, herself, tried not to watch, too. Only when it was midnight did Paul give up hope and agree to Yvonne's suggestion that he should take her home.

That night he made love to her and there were tears on Yvonne's lashes as she settled down at last to an exhausted sleep; tears that Paul neither saw nor would have cared about for each knew that he had not really been making love to Yvonne at all.

★ ★ ★ ★

He had found her without difficulty on the nursery slopes. He had been out watching the skiers for her since breakfast.

'Mademoiselle Ann!' he greeted her as he came to a spectacular Christie stop in a flurry of snow beside her. 'I have been looking for you. I think perhaps you have an explanation for me?'

Ann smiled.

'I hoped I'd see you this morning!' she admitted. 'It wasn't possible for me to explain properly last night on the phone.'

Anxiously, she gave him her prepared version of what had happened after her return from the Point. She refrained from saying that the Mentons were particularly anxious she did not go out with *him!* But Paul said it for her.

'I warned you, Ann, that there were

people who would try to put you against me. It does not surprise me. Of course, I was very hurt when you said you could not come. I had been so much looking forward to our evening.'

'I had, too!' Ann cried. 'And believe me, Paul, if it had been my own wish, I would have come. But you must see that it was awkward for me as I live with the Mentons. I can't totally disregard their wishes.'

'I am not blaming you!' Paul said, covering her gloved hand with his. 'But it does seem unfair if I am not to be permitted to see you.'

'Oh, we can meet like this!' Ann said consolingly. 'It's just that I can't have an evening date with you till my mother writes back to Madame Menton. I've asked her to do so by airmail the moment she gets my letter so it shouldn't be long.'

'And you think your mother will agree?'

'But of course!' Ann said. 'My mother knows she can trust me to be sensible.'

'Even with someone as bad as me?'

Ann knew he was teasing.

'I don't think you're all that bad, Paul. I think you just want me to think you are!'

Now Paul was no longer smiling.

'On the contrary, Ann, I wish you to

think only good of me. I would give much indeed to be able to wipe away this bad reputation I have. It is most important to me that you should like and respect me.'

'But I do!' Ann argued. 'I've told you already, Paul, I'll make my own judgements. I don't care what the Mentons say about you. I'll go on seeing you as often as I please!'

'Ah, you have courage as well as beauty!' Paul said. 'Well, then, show me a little more of it, Ann, and tell me you will spend this afternoon with me.'

'Up to the Point again?' Ann asked, excited in spite of her determination to stay calm and collected.

'No, I had thought I might take you elsewhere, where we could be more by ourselves. There are too many people on the Point! I cannot kiss you in front of such crowds.'

Had Paul been one of the boys at home, Ann would have replied tartly: 'And how do you know I want to be kissed? But she felt such a remark would seem ridiculous to Paul.

He watched her rising colour and said casually:

'We can take the cable car to the

Merveille stop. From there, there is a little path I know to a wooden cabin. It is really a kind of woodcutter's hut but it is used only very occasionally, by climbers or skiers who are injured or have lost their way. I thought it might be amusing to take a little picnic with us and we could sit in the sunshine and lean against the walls of the hut and get sunburned. Would you enjoy this?'

At first Paul's suggestion of the isolated wooden chalet had shaken Ann's self-confidence. Suppose, she thought, everything said about Paul was true and she couldn't trust him? To put herself in a lonely place where she could not call for help would be asking for trouble!

But even as the thought flashed through her mind, she rejected it as absurd. Paul was hardly likely to try and rape her! And she could well fend off any other advances. Anyway, it was quite ridiculous to be thinking in such terms at all. Paul had perfectly frankly expressed desire to be alone with her so that he could kiss her. Moreover, he was talking about picnics and sunbathing. She was letting Luc and his mother affect her judgement! They almost

194

had her believing he really was as bad as they painted.

'I'd love it!' she said truthfully. 'It'll make up for missing our dancing last night.'

'I was so unhappy!' Paul told her. 'I kept hoping you might come to the club, with Luc perhaps, so that I could dance at least once with you. Were you at home then?'

Ann told him about the cinema. Paul frowned.

'I am most jealous of Luc!' he said as she finished. 'He has so many advantages over me. Not only does he live under the same roof, but he is young and has no evil reputation to live down!'

Ann laughed.

'I don't think you should take your reputation so seriously,' she said consolingly. 'I'm not, so why should you?'

'Because I would like to be like Luc—to be sure that you would never turn against me because of what others say. You like him, do you not? Perhaps even love him a little?'

Ann's eyes danced. It was fun to think of Paul a little jealous.

'Of course I like him—he's very nice!'

'Ah, you are teasing me. But you do not say you love him so I will not be angry with you. Ann—such a pretty name and you are so pretty. You cannot imagine how much I have been thinking of you. All night long I could not sleep for thoughts of you. I am already caring far too much for you. You know that?'

Ann felt a return of her confusion. His words excited and confused her at once. She wanted him to care and yet she was not sure of her own feelings.

'Please tell me that you care a little for me, too?' he was pleading. She decided to be non-committal.

'A little!' she said lightly. 'But you mustn't be so serious on a lovely morning like this. Will you show me how to do those Christie turns? Luc has not come to give me my lesson today so I need an instructor. I was making no progress on my own.'

She had been a little hurt if not altogether surprised by Luc's announcement at breakfast that he must work on his father's accounts that morning. She had half expected him not to ski with her. But she had been disappointed all the same, even although she realised it would give her a better chance of meeting and talking to Paul. Now that Paul was here with her, she forgot her annoyance with Luc and was glad he was absent. She was sure he didn't really have to do Monsieur Menton's accounts that morning and was just trying to show her that he could be as independent as she was. When she told him Paul had given her her ski-ing instruction, he would be sorry he hadn't come!

But in the end, she did not mention Paul at lunch. She was afraid lest Luc or his mother might ask her outright if she had made a further date with Paul that afternoon. She was wondering what excuse she would make if Luc offered to accompany her on the nursery slopes, but he did not do so.

'I'm going to have a couple of runs down from the Point,' he announced over coffee. 'It should be perfect today. I'll see you all later.'

Just for an instant, Ann wished fervently that she were as good a skier as Luc and could go with him. It would, indeed, be a perfect afternoon to ski down from the Point. The snow was firm and the sky cloudless. But then she forgot the wish in the pleasurable anticipation of going to meet Paul.

Unlike the changeable English spring weather, the sky remained a brilliant blue as Ann set off after lunch. The air, though cold, was summer-like with the heat of the sun's rays. Only in the shadows did she feel at all cold although she was wearing only a thin jersey and carried her anorak. Her face, in the manner of all the other young people, was without make-up and covered in sun oil.

Paul gave her a quick, admiring glance as they met at the foot of the cable car lift. He tucked his arm in hers. He had a small rucksack slung across his shoulders, which, he told her, contained a thermos of coffee, a bottle of wine and some fruit.

'I've just eaten an enormous lunch!' Ann said. 'I'll never be able to eat anything more.'

But Paul assured her it wouldn't be long before the mountain air gave her a fresh appetite—and a thirst.

He had also brought a small waterproof square which served them as a groundsheet when finally they reached the hut and picked a sunny place against the south wall. The snow there was thick and soft and the waterproof very necessary as they sat down and leaned their backs against the wooden building.

There was no one else in sight. They were above the tree line and except for the dripping of the melting snow from the roof, there was no sound other than that of their own voices.

'It's perfect!' Ann said, letting her head rest against the wall, closing her eyes against the sun as she removed her dark glasses. 'Almost too hot!'

Suddenly, she felt Paul's mouth on her own. Then his arms went round her shoulders, drawing her forward against him. It was the first time he had kissed her and Ann's reactions frightened her. She sensed his pent-up intensity of desire and knew that her body was beginning to respond to him even whilst her mind rejected this kind of kissing.

'No!' she whispered as he drew his mouth away for a moment. 'No, Paul.'

But his lips came back hard to hers as if he had not heard her. Against her will, she began to return his kisses. The white world around them disappeared as she closed her eyes, blotting out the hard, glittering desire she could read in Paul's face; obliterating everything but the feel of his mouth, his lips and her own violent trembling.

When at last he let her go, she all but fell back against the wall. Her breath was coming in deep uneven gasps and she raised her hands instinctively to push against Paul's chest as he bent over her.

'Do not be afraid. I shan't hurt you!' he told her, his voice husky and uneven.

But it was not so much Paul she feared as the violence of her own feelings. She wanted him to kiss her again, to go on kissing her. She wanted...

'Ann, I love you. Do you hear me? I love you and I want you desperately. I am torn with longing for you.'

The pressure of her hands against him relaxed slightly. At once he began to kiss her again. This time she succeeded with a great effort of will, in turning her head away.

'No, Paul! This...this won't help either of us. I...please let's stop. When you are kissing me like that, I can't think!'

'But you feel!' Paul said triumphantly, 'as I feel. I want you, Ann, and you want me, don't you? Your body tells me what your lips deny.'

'That's the trouble!' Ann said. 'Somehow, when you kiss me that way, I don't seem to have any control left.'

'You must not be afraid of love,' Paul said quickly. Gently, he reached out his hands and began to caress her. Ann felt her limbs melt slowly, magically, beneath his touch.

'I must stop this. I must!' she thought, but she could not bring herself to push his hands away.

'Love is wonderful, beautiful, exciting!' Paul murmured, his face so close to hers that she could feel his breath hot against her cheeks. 'Let me love you, Ann.'

'But, Paul, we can't be sure what we feel is love!' she cried. 'This...this is...'

'Desire?' Paul asked softly. 'Then I desire you, Ann. I love you. I want you. You cannot deny yourself to me.'

'But I don't want to make love!' The words were out at last. Now she did manage to raise her arms and hold his hands away from her. 'Please don't touch me like that again, Paul. I suppose it sounds silly to you, but I don't want to make love. Not until I'm absolutely sure I'm in love. Can't you understand? I could say yes and in a way it would be true

because I want you to go on doing what you were doing. I want you the same way you want me. But I'd be sorry afterwards. I know I would. Then I'd hate you.'

With a stupendous effort, Paul controlled himself. He was tempted to ignore her words; to make her want him enough to forget all her scruples or morals or ideals, whichever it was that she was putting between them. But her last sentence held him in check. He did not want her to hate him afterwards. He would be gentle, tender, considerate with her. He would love her as no other man would love her.

'Don't you trust me?' he asked. 'Don't you care how I feel, Ann? Don't you see how terrible it is, knowing you do want me as I want you and yet denying ourselves so much joy? Don't you believe I love you?'

She looked into his face and wondered how one could be sure if the look in a man's eyes when he wanted you was love or just desire? She wasn't old enough or experienced enough to know. She only knew how *she* felt and she was *not* sure she loved him.

'I doubt myself!' she cried. 'I'm not sure of anything any more, Paul. Only that I don't want this to go any further.'

He looked directly into her eyes, his own half angry, half tender.

'You are afraid!' he said. 'Afraid of love—or of me. Well, you shall see that I love you well enough. I will not touch you again although I could very easily make you love me, Ann.'

Was it a threat? Ann was suddenly reminded of Luc's warning—'He is not to be trusted!' But that was ridiculous. Paul had just promised he would not touch her unless she wished it.

She put out her hand and brushed the hair from her eyes in a childish gesture of confusion.

'I'm sorry, Paul!' she whispered. 'You must be thinking me very young and silly.'

With a deep sigh, Paul drew back from her and lit a cigarette.

'I am the one who is silly!' he said as he breathed in the smoke. 'I had hoped you cared.'

'Don't be angry!' Ann begged. 'All I'm asking for is a little time, Paul—time to get to know you better; to know myself better. I...I've never had a love affair before. I've never even thought seriously about it. I suppose there's never been anyone I found sufficiently attractive to want to let them make love to me. You...you are the first, Paul.'

He was instantly mollified. He leant back and drew her sideways against him so that she rested in the circle of his arm.

'There!' he said. 'That is more comfortable, no?'

She knew that the moment of temptation and danger had passed for the time being and allowed herself to relax. Now Luc's warning seemed even sillier. *Of course* Paul was to be trusted. She was foolish ever to have been afraid that he would be unwilling to take no for an answer.

'What we both need is a drink!'

Paul's voice was quite calm, matter of fact. He seemed willing to forget the whole incident.

'It is so hot in the sun. I'm glad I thought to put the wine to chill in the snow.'

It was on the tip of Ann's tongue to say that she did not want any wine. She didn't care for the taste and she wasn't used to drinking in mid-afternoon. But she bit back the words. As it was, Paul must be thinking her behaviour gauche and adolescent. She must try to retrieve some semblance of sophistication.

Forcing an answering smile to her lips, she took the glass from him and imitating his gesture, gulped it down.

11

Luc, on his way to the post office, lost in thought, nearly bumped into the young woman approaching him.

'Oh, Marie, I'm so sorry!' he apologised, smiling at her. 'My fault entirely. I wasn't looking where I was going.'

'So I noticed!' Marie replied. 'Well, Luc, how goes it?'

She was herself returning from the coiffeur where she had had her raven dark hair dressed in a new style on top of her head. It suited her and she knew that she looked her best. Running into Luc was quite accidental but fortuitous. For once he was not in the company of the English girl, Ann.

'All right, I suppose,' Luc replied so half-heartedly that it was obvious to Marie everything was far from well with his world. He looked and sounded depressed. She could guess why. She knew where and with whom Ann was this afternoon. Small wonder Luc was fed up.

'How about standing me a cup of coffee?' she asked. 'I have just been to the hairdresser and I am thirsty from the heat.'

Luc hesitated. He did not really want to accompany Marie but on the other hand he had nothing to do when he returned home. He should have kept his lunch-time plan to go ski-ing on the Point but there had been no enthusiasm for the idea since he would not have Ann with him. Somehow, he was unable to enjoy anything any more without her there beside him. He knew very well that his love was unwelcome to her. Hurt and confused by her attitude to him and Duret, he had decided that the best course of action would be to pick up the threads of his life where he had left them on Ann's arrival in Aiguille. He would live as if she did not exist—leaving her to run her own life as she chose.

It was proving one thing to plan such an intention and another to carry it out. He had watched her leave the house this morning to go off for her morning ski-ing, with a mixture of emotions. She looked so young and defenceless and she was having difficulty shouldering the skis which, usually, he carried for her. One part of him was sorely tempted to rush down and help her and to offer to go with her. But the other part of him, hurt, stood on his pride. Let her go alone! Maybe she was going to meet Duret anyway. It was her business. He wasn't going to interfere; force his company on her. She had justly accused him of being jealous so she must know how much he cared about her and she had shown him he meant nothing to her. He would now make her see that she meant as little to him!

In this mood, he had announced at lunch that he had firm plans for the afternoon. He had been further hurt when no signs of disappointment appeared on her face. If anything at all, she looked relieved. He was so upset by her indifference that he lost heart for the ski-ing and stayed home to complete the work his father had asked him to do. He had watched Ann leave the house without her skis. A casual question to his mother had received the reply that Ann had not told anyone where she was going. He could draw only one conclusion—that she was meeting Paul Duret again.

'Well?' Marie was asking with a hint of impatience. 'Are you going to stand me a cup of coffee, Luc?'

He nodded, unable to elicit any enthusiasm into his voice as he said:

'Where shall we go? Annabelle's?'

Being mid-afternoon and the weather fine, the majority of people were out ski-ing so the café was more or less empty. They found a corner table without difficulty and coffee was brought to them.

'You're very quiet!' Marie commented after a moment or two during which Luc was lost in thought. 'Or else in love?'

The barb hit home. Luc's face coloured and he looked up at the girl beside him and quickly away again.

'It's the English girl, Ann, of course!' Marie said with a hint of bitterness in her tone. 'Come on, Luc, you might as well admit it to me. We are friends since childhood. Surely you don't have to pretend to me?'

'That's true, I suppose!' Luc agreed. Suddenly he remembered that his mother had once told him Marie would have been very happy to have had a proposal from him. He felt vaguely uncomfortable at the memory. He had never been in the least in love with her although he thought her attractive enough and likeable, too, in a rather hot-headed, passionate but sincere way. Her temperament was very Italian. He found her a little too domineering and forceful. But he stayed friendly with her and now, he felt the need to talk. It would be a relief to be able to tell someone how he felt!

'Tell me the truth, Luc. You are in love with this girl?'

'Yes!' said Luc, stirring the spoon round and round in his cup with unseeing eyes. 'I love her so much that I don't know how I can face living day in and day out knowing she is not for me.'

Marie's eyebrows rose in a quick, uncontrolled movement.

'Oh, it's possible to live in such fashion!' she said with a bitter note in her voice. 'We can grow to accept anything in time. You have not known her very long, Luc. You will get over it!'

'No!' he said in a disconcertingly firm voice. 'This is for keeps, Marie. I know it must sound silly. It's true that I haven't known Ann for long. But long enough to be quite sure that I love her; that she's the one girl in the world I want to marry.'

Marie let out her breath on a long sigh. How unfair life was! She herself had been willing to give Luc a lifelong devotion;

had loved him for years and years, yet he cared nothing at all for her. Then he met a girl and in a matter of days, decided he wanted to marry her. It wasn't reasonable. Yet deep down, she could see what there was in Ann that so attracted Luc. She, herself, had wanted to dislike the girl; had approached her in the most unfriendly manner and left ten minutes later actually liking her.

'Maybe you will marry her one day? When she has grown up a little!' Marie said astutely. What she really meant was 'after the affair with Paul has run its course'. She had no doubt that Ann *would* have an affair with Paul. Paul always got what he wanted. It depended whether Luc would ever be able to overlook the indiscretion; the crack in his idol's perfection; whether he loved Ann enough to want her when Paul had finished with her. Luc was an idealist. Because of this, she could still hope Luc might turn to her, for she could not see him accepting Paul Duret's discarded mistress for his wife!

'Ann is not in love with me!' Luc was saying miserably. 'I mean nothing at all to her. It is quite obvious that she prefers...older men!'

'You mean, an older man!' Marie said gently. 'Why pretend, Luc? We both know she is fascinated by Paul Duret!'

Luc gave her a quick anxious look.

'How do you know that? Just because she went up to the Point with him yesterday, you are jumping to conclusions.'

Marie's voice was almost sympathetic now.

'Luc, if I am jumping to conclusions, they are ones you yourself must have reached. Besides, apart from yesterday afternoon, what about *this* afternoon?'

She assumed that Ann had told Luc where she was going in the same way that Paul had triumphantly announced to her over lunch-time drinks at the bar, that he was taking Ann up to the hut above Merveille. It was well known locally to be an isolated and ideal spot for lovers to meet where they could count on not being surrounded by other people.

Luc hesitated. He did not want to have to ask Marie where Ann was. He realised she knew and that it must be somewhere with Paul. But where? He hoped very much it would be the Point again. There at least she had the protection of the crowds.

'I'm sure Ann is quite old enough to look after herself!' he said stiffly, the lie coming with difficulty. 'It is no concern of mine how she chooses to spend her afternoon.'

Marie shrugged.

'If you really loved her, Luc, as you said, you can't be all that indifferent to her fate. After all, she *is* very young and Paul can be very persuasive. Besides, perhaps she wants an affair with him. She may not be quite as pure as you seem to think.'

Marie's words sent a shock of apprehension through Luc. He looked at her almost with hatred.

'You don't know Ann or you wouldn't talk about her like that!' he said furiously. 'She may be attracted to Paul Duret but she would no more think of having an affair with him than...than you!'

Marie's eyebrows rose sarcastically.

'Then she's certainly behaving very oddly,' she said coolly. 'I mean, anyone with a grain of common sense knows that the Merveille hut is the place to go if you want a little privacy. Surely even Ann with all her so-called innocence, can't imagine Paul would be content with a kiss or two?'

She was unprepared for the vice-like grip Luc now fastened on her arm.

'The Merveille hut?' he repeated. 'What makes you say they are there? How do you know? Answer me, Marie!'

She was suddenly frightened. She had never seen such violence in Luc before. She realised now that he had been quite unaware of Ann's whereabouts and wished desperately that she had kept her mouth shut.

'If you don't tell me at once, Marie, I'll...'

'Paul told me he was taking her there!' The words came out sullenly. 'I'm sorry, Luc. I thought you knew. Anyway, it has nothing to do with me. I'm not Ann's keeper.'

Luc let go her arm and stood up, staring down at her as if he were quite unaware of her as a person.

'I've got to go up there. She won't have realised. She doesn't know about people like Duret.'

Now Marie was really concerned. She, too, stood up and laid a restraining hand on Luc's arm.

'You can't go up there!' she said. 'It can't do any good. If she wishes to be there alone with Paul, you can't stop her. She'd hate you for bursting in on them if...and even if as you say, she doesn't realise what it's all about, she'd not going to let you interfere. Anyway, I know Paul. He might try to seduce her but he won't rape her, if that's what's worrying you.'

Luc's expression was now truly murderous.

'If he's touched her, I'll kill him. I'm not leaving her alone up there with him. She won't know anything about the Merveille hut. She won't know anything about a man like Duret, either. I'm going up there.'

'Luc, be reasonable, you...'

But her words were lost for he had already turned and hurried out of the café, his agitation so great that he had even forgotten to pay the bill.

She pushed a note under her coffee cup and hurried out into the street after Luc. She was forced to run to catch up with him.

'If you're going, let me come with you. It would look more natural if we went together—as if we didn't realise they were there,' she pleaded. 'If everything is okay, you can pretend you did not expect them to be there!'

216

Luc's pace slowed. It was a reasonable suggestion. He had automatically assumed the worst but if Ann were perfectly all right, he would indeed look extremely foolish bursting upon them like a Victorian husband after an erring wife! Ann would hate him.

'That's very nice of you, Marie!' he said more gently. 'But Duret knows you knew he was going there. He'll know it wasn't an accidental meeting.'

Marie sighed.

'Certainly! I'll make an enemy for life but at least *you* won't have to look a complete idiot to *Ann.*'

'That's very nice of you!' Luc said again.

'You can remember me in your will!' Marie retorted frivolously. But privately her heart was aching. She had acted on impulse. Her love for Luc had prompted the wish to protect him. She had put him first, as she always would. But it wouldn't help to make him love her. Moreover, she might be saving the situation for him with Ann. She must, she told herself, be out of her mind.

Luc would not wait for further discussion. Already he was striding up the hill towards the cable car lift to Merveille and she was well aware that he would stop for nothing. She hurried to keep up with him.

His silence gave her time to reflect on the situation. At best it would not be a very enjoyable encounter. Paul would be absolutely furious with her for betraying a confidence. But then he had not made any secret of his intentions. He'd been all but boasting of it to her. He'd given her the impression that it was only a matter of time before he'd overcome Ann's resistance. She had not doubted it. She'd never seen Paul so taken with a girl that he was prepared to do the chasing. Usually it was the other way round! But perhaps it was Ann's unobtainability that attracted him.

She tried to visualise Ann's reactions to a man like Paul. Obviously she was very unsophisticated and probably hadn't met anyone like him before. Would he frighten her? Or would he succeed in charming her? Paul could be more charming than anyone Marie knew when he chose. But would a girl like Ann be willing to have an affair? Marie knew that teenage English girls were said to be very promiscuous these days; that they lived in a free, permissive society where love-making at will was accepted and expected. She had seen the way some of the young girls who came to Aiguille behaved. Why then, imagine that Ann was different?

Yet Marie felt instinctively that Ann *was* different. There was a freshness, an innocence that proclaimed her the ingénue. Luc sensed it, too.'

'Perhaps not any longer!' Marie thought as she and Luc sat side by side in the two-seater cabin, being carried higher and higher up the mountainside towards Merveille.

She shivered, suddenly anxious and afraid of what Luc might do if they found Ann really in need of help! He looked so tense and strung up that a tiny fear ran down her spine. Like a lot of quiet, unviolent men, Luc had a streak in him that could burst through his normal self-control. Then, and only then, he could show a greater violence than the kind of man whose emotions were nearer the surface. She had once seen Luc provoked beyond endurance into a fight with a boy at school. His aggressor was older, stronger and fearless, yet when finally a master managed to prise the boys apart, the bigger boy had been so badly beaten he'd had to go to the doctor for several stitches in his head.

If Luc could half-kill someone when he was only a boy, what might not happen now that he was a man—and a man who was emotionally disturbed by love?

She began to wish fervently that she had stayed at the coiffeur a little longer and never run into Luc in the manner which had seemed so fortuitous at the time. Now she could see it only as the most unlucky stroke of Fate.

12

'Well, goodness me, if it isn't Luc!'

Ann giggled but did not move from her position half lying across Paul's lap. An empty glass lay beside her. In one hand she held the now empty bottle of wine. The other lay slackly beside her.

Paul shifted uncomfortably beneath her and tried to help her to a more upright position. But Ann was slack, dead weight. There could be little doubt about the fact that she was tight.

'Aren't you going to say hullo?' Ann went on, the only one of the four of them who seemed able to find her voice. 'Why doesn't someone say something. Marie? Aren't you going to say hullo to us? We're having a wonderful, wonderful picnic and...' A hiccough made her forget the rest of what she had been about to say. She felt sleepy and dizzy and very, very content. She tried to slide back down onto Paul's lap but suddenly, he stood up, leaving her sprawled on the groundsheet.

Luc, who had been stunned to immobility by the sight of Ann lying in so helpless and abandoned a position, now stepped forward and grabbed Paul's arm.

'She's tight!' he said in rapid French. 'You've been pouring wine down her all afternoon, haven't you, you...'

He let out a stream of insulting names which left Marie gasping. Quickly, she stepped forward to intervene.

'That's not fair, Luc. Ann may have chosen to drink of her own free will. You can't blame Paul when...'

'You be quiet!' Luc turned on her, silencing her in mid-sentence. His eyes were blazing and his face was grey-white as Ann, quite oblivious to the tension above her, reached up the bottle and offered Luc a drink.

'Get up!' he said. 'Now, this minute. We are going home.'

The smile faded from Ann's face.

'But I don't want to go home. I'm having a lovely, lovely, lovely time. I want to stay here with Paul. I...'

'Get up!' Luc said harshly. He bent down and pulled Ann upright. She closed her eyes, swaying against him.

'Funny, I feel dizzy!' she said stupidly.

'I don't think I'm feeling very well.'

She tried to lie down again but Luc held her in a vice-like grip. Ann turned to Paul.

'Why don't you tell him to let me go!' she complained. 'Tell Luc to go away, Paul. I want to stay here in the sun with you!'

Once again Marie tried to intervene. She went to Ann's side and said softly and persuasively:

'You must come home with us, Ann. It's time we went back. The party is over.'

Now, at last, Paul found his voice. With an attempt at nonchalance, he said:

'Perhaps you two would consider minding your own business? You heard what Ann said, Menton. Now, go!'

Luc gave him a withering look, filled with contempt.

'Are you seriously suggesting I leave her here with you, drunk and quite incapable of defending herself?'

'Defending herself!' Paul repeated, flushing an angry red. 'I think you have stepped out of line, Menton. I have not and would not harm a hair of Ann's head. I love her. I intend to marry her.'

Luc's mouth fell open. Of all the things

Duret might have said, he had not expected this. He looked quickly at Ann.

'Is that true?' he asked.

She gazed at him wide-eyed.

'Is what true? I wish you wouldn't look so cross, Luc. I don't like it when you're angry.'

He drew in his breath sharply.

'Listen to me, Ann. Pay attention. *I want to know if it's true you intend to marry Duret. Has Paul asked you to marry him?*'

Ann frowned. She honestly did not know what Luc was talking about.

'I like Paul!' she announced. 'He's nice. And I like you, too, Luc, so long as you aren't cross.'

Luc realised that Ann's concentration was not up to taking an intelligent part in the conversation. He turned back to Paul.

'Well, have you proposed to her? Did Ann accept? I find that as hard to believe as that you haven't taken advantage of her. I know you, Duret. I wouldn't trust you further than I can see you.'

Calmly, Paul reached for a packet of cigarettes and slowly lit one.

'I really don't see how this concerns you in any way, Menton. Ann is not your property. Nor have you any right to interfere in my life. I'd appreciate it if you would mind your own business.'

Luc lost his temper.

'You deliberately got her drunk!' he raged. 'And if you've so much as touched her, I'll...'

'Luc!' Marie stepped quickly between the two men. 'This isn't the time to talk. We should get Ann home. I don't think she's feeling too well!'

A quick glance at Ann's pale face brought Luc back to a semblance of control.

He pushed past Paul and took Ann's arm. She said weakly:

'I think I've had too much sun. I'm feeling sick!'

Paul moved as if to intervene, but Marie put a hand on his arm and said:

'Best let her go, Paul. I know Luc. He won't leave without her and there'll only be a scene. Give him best now. You can do what you want later.'

Paul looked down at her bitterly.

'I thought you were a friend of mine, Marie. You *told* him we were here. You were the only one who knew.'

'I couldn't help it,' Marie said. 'I honestly thought Luc knew.'

'Well, don't think this little episode is

going to do you any good!' Paul said cruelly. 'Luc obviously doesn't give a damn whether you even exist.'

Now Marie's eyes were bitter.

'I know he loves her but it doesn't stop me loving him.'

'And a fat lot of good that will do you!' Paul said cruelly. 'If you think he'll change his mind about her now, you're very much mistaken.'

'He might!' Marie said thoughtfully, although the idea had not struck her until now. 'Luc thought Ann was perfect. After this, his ideal will be somewhat shattered, especially if things did go as far as he seems to think.'

'I did not make love to her!' Paul said in an undertone. 'What kind of a man do you think I am that I would get a girl drunk and then force her against her will?'

'Perhaps, if she were drunk enough, it wouldn't be against her will!' Marie replied calmly.

Paul flushed.

'I didn't know she had no head for wine. A drink or two shouldn't have brought her to this state. It's ridiculous!'

'For a young girl who doesn't normally drink, I would say half a bottle of wine was more than sufficient!' Marie retorted.

By now, Luc was already some distance along the path, supporting Ann who seemed unable to keep her feet. It was as well they hadn't far to go to the cabin halt, Marie thought. She doubted if Ann would have made it.

As Paul turned away to gather up the remains of the picnic paraphernalia, she watched him with narrowed eyes. What a fool he was to behave in such a way. Luc would not let the matter drop here. He might have no right to interfere in Ann's life but his parents had, since Ann was in their care. Ann was still a minor. If Paul had touched her, they could bring a case against him for assault. Not that Marie felt such a thing likely. They would not want the publicity for themselves, for Ann, for the club. What had possessed Paul to act so indiscreetly? Was he really in love with Ann? Had he meant it when he said he intended to marry her? And if so, what would Madame Verdos have to say? And what of Ann's parents? If they knew Paul's reputation, they could never permit such a marriage.

'You would be wisest not to see her any more,' she told Paul as they moved off down the path in Luc's wake. 'Any other way will spell trouble, Paul, with a capital T.'

'I have nothing to fear!' Paul said sharply. 'I am in love with the girl, Marie. I want her and I intend to have her. I'm going to marry her.'

'That is ridiculous,' Marie argued. 'You must know perfectly well that such a marriage would not be acceptable. Apart from the difference in your ages, can you believe Ann's parents will overlook your past, Paul? And don't pretend innocence to *me*.'

'I will wait until she is old enough to go against her parents' wishes,' Paul said. 'She is nearly nineteen. In two years' time she can choose for herself.'

'Then you think *she* loves *you?*'

Paul looked away from Marie's eyes, his own evasive.

'Not yet, perhaps. But I could make her love me.'

Luc and Ann had already reached the halt. With only twenty yards or so before they caught up with them, Marie said:

'You must have been mad, Paul, getting her drunk. Or was that your intention? Surely you realised what people would think when she returned home in this condition? Babbling away about how she liked kissing you! Or was that your idea—to make people think the worst had happened? To compromise her so that you could produce a valid and noble reason for wanting to marry her?'

'I had no set plan!' Paul said harshly. 'Anyway, I was not to know you would bring Luc up here after us.'

'In fact, Luc brought me!' she said. 'But although I never for a moment imagined my careless talk would produce these results, I must say I'm beginning to think it was just as well we did come.'

Ignoring Paul's half-hearted protests, Luc acted as if he was not there and climbed into the first empty cabin taking Ann with him. She seemed to have forgotten Paul and looked as if she might fall asleep at any moment. Regarding her, Marie suddenly appreciated why Luc was so angry. The girl was only a kid! Without make-up, her hair boyish and dishevelled, her face in a dreamy repose, Ann could pass for fifteen. Even at eighteen, Marie reflected, a girl who had led a sheltered life could still be very young and innocent. Marie could see now that Ann's sophistication was only a pose. Underneath the façade, she was still very much a child.

As she climbed into the second cabin, her thoughts turned again to Paul who sat opposite her in sulky silence. It was so very unlike him to have behaved with such indiscretion. But then, as far as she knew, Paul had never made a pass at so young a girl before. Mostly, the women he found to amuse him were well aware of what was in store for them when they went off alone with him; they were as ready to enjoy themselves as Paul.

It was possible he really had had no idea that this quantity of alcohol could so affect someone not accustomed to drinking. On the other hand, her earlier theory could have been true—that he had meant to compromise Ann. This would give him the excuse for breaking with Yvonne Verdos—and he *would* need an excuse after all these years. Marie could not imagine that such a very long-standing affair could be ended easily, even if the older woman was prepared to let Paul go without a fuss.

She gave an involuntary shiver of disgust. Luc was perfectly right—this wasn't the kind of set-up in which a girl like Ann should be involved. This was quite unfitting and the thought of Ann married to a man like Paul was almost revolting. The years had made Marie fairly easy-going in her attitude to life and other people's morals even if she did not subscribe to them herself, but she knew that if Ann were her sister instead of her rival, she would be protecting her from Paul with all the means at her disposal.

Back at Aiguille, Luc and Ann had already disembarked and were walking home without stopping for Paul and Marie. A little hurt that Luc had at least not stayed to thank her, Marie sighed and shrugged her shoulders.

'*Au revoir*, then, Paul!' she said. 'Let's hope Luc lets this whole unfortunate episode drop here. I advise you to do the same. Not that you will take my advice. But if you do try to see Ann alone again, I think you will have trouble with the Menton family.'

'I am not afraid of trouble,' Paul stated. 'And I have every intention of seeing Ann again as long as she wishes to see me. If Luc should ask, you can tell him I said so.'

Marie walked off, cold, tired and depressed. The afternoon had been quite meaningless for her. Luc bore her no gratitude for her part in rescuing Ann. It might well have been better for her if she had left Ann to her fate!

But she knew she couldn't really have acted any differently once Luc had decided he was going to find Ann. She would never be able to turn her back on him when he needed help, not even when she was acting against her own self-interests.

'Such,' she told herself bitterly, 'is the price of love.'

★ ★ ★ ★

'Ann is not feeling well, Maman!' Luc said as they entered the house and he helped her off with her anorak. 'I think she should go straight to bed. Too much sun...' he added vaguely.

'I don't want to go to bed...' Ann began but Luc silenced her with:

'Do as I say, Ann. Maman will bring you some coffee in a minute.'

With some difficulty, Ann negotiated the stairs. Madame Menton watched for a moment and then followed Luc into the

232

kitchen, her face concerned.

'What is wrong, Luc?' she asked as she put the big copper kettle on the range. 'Is she ill?'

'She is drunk!' Luc said, his anger now free to express itself. 'She will be all right when she has slept it off.'

Something in Luc's voice caused his mother to look up at him anxiously, controlling the protest that had risen to her lips at his announcement.

'What is wrong, Luc?' she asked gently. 'Do you wish to tell me?'

Luc hesitated. His mother was a practical, sensible woman with ordinary principles and opinions about life. She would be as angry as he when she heard Paul Duret's part in this but she would also be extremely angry with Ann. She might even send her back to England. In a way, Ann had betrayed her trust. She had promised his mother not to go out with Paul last night yet had gone off alone with him this afternoon. At best, it was splitting hairs. The time of day would make little enough difference to Paul Duret!

Had it prevented him from making love to Ann? he thought wildly. The question, held until now at the back of his mind, hit him with full force. He could not bear the thought. He almost hated Ann at that moment. If only he could answer himself with total certainty—no, she's not like that!

But he wasn't sure. That was the hell of it. His mother would want to know, too. No, he couldn't tell her the truth. He must protect Ann. At least, if she had done anything wrong, no one else should know it.

'I'm afraid I gave her too much wine!' Luc lied, not meeting his mother's eyes. 'It was very silly of me. Now, I regret to say, Ann is drunk. She did not realise the wine was so strong and, stupidly, I did not stop her after one glass.'

Madame Menton did not for one instant believe him. She knew her son very well; knew that he would never behave in such a fashion. But equally, she knew that if he did not wish to tell her what had really happened, wild horses would not drag the truth out of him. Wisely she did not press him. She made coffee and told Luc to take it up to Ann.

'No!' His reply was so forceful that once again his mother shot him an anxious glance. 'No, you take it!' Luc said with an effort to remain calm. He didn't want to see Ann—couldn't bear to hear her say again, in that drowsy, childish voice: 'I like Paul kissing me!'

'I shouldn't ask her any questions just now,' he added. 'I think her replies might not make much sense.'

'So he doesn't want me to question her!' Madame Menton thought. 'Whatever has happened, Luc is ashamed.'

She knew then for a certainty that Luc was in love with Ann. She had suspected it these last few days and even been quite happy to think that at last he was taking a girl seriously again. She liked Ann and so did her husband. From all accounts, she came of good family and if anything developed from the friendship, she would have nothing against such a marriage. But she knew Ann was not in the least in love with Luc, and Madame Menton did not want him hurt. She would not permit anyone to hurt her son.

As she climbed the stairs to Ann's room, it crossed her mind that she could always send Ann back to England if all did not go well between the young people. Luc was her first concern and no girl, however nice, was going to upset him if she could avoid it.

She decided to ignore Luc's request and ask Ann if they had quarrelled; what had brought her to this unhappy state. But when she opened the door of Ann's room, Ann was in bed and already fast asleep.

13

Ann woke the following morning with a violent headache. Remembering a little of what had happened the afternoon before, she decided that she was experiencing her first hangover. She felt hot, feverish and very, very ashamed. She was also furious with Luc for coming up the mountain to find her as if she was an errant schoolgirl who could not be trusted out alone.

But by the time she had washed and dressed, she felt too ill to worry about Luc or Paul or anything but the terrible pain in her head and the agonising soreness of her throat.

In a matter of hours, Ann was back in bed again, diagnosed by the doctor as suffering from acute tonsillitis. She was to take antibiotics four-hourly and to rest as much as possible.

For two days her temperature remained high enough for her to be only semi-conscious. She was aware of Madame Menton's skilled nursing and kindly face as she brought medicine and cool drinks and remade Ann's crumpled bed. For the rest of the time, she was tormented by violent dreams, sometimes of Paul, sometimes of Luc. In one of these nightmares, she was running away from Paul, terrified because she knew he intended her harm. In another she was lost on the mountains, searching for Luc who had promised to come and find her but never arrived. In a third, Paul was kissing her and she alternatively struggled against him and tried to draw him closer. Then his features changed and became so evil and frightening that she was terrified, wanting to run away yet unable to move. Slowly his features dissolved and changed yet again and the face became Luc's and the fear disappeared.

She woke from such dreams utterly exhausted.

When finally her temperature began to drop, she had lost a lot of weight, looked thin and pale, the golden suntan she had acquired changed to an unattractive sallowness.

She admitted to Madame Menton that she felt awful.

'Nevertheless, the doctor said this morning you are beginning to improve!' Madame said cheerfully. 'How is the throat?'

'Still rather sore!' Ann said hoarsely. 'I'm so very sorry, Madame, to have caused you all this trouble. I simply can't understand why I should have got tonsillitis out here in this climate. I have had occasional bouts at home but my own doctor seemed to think the Swiss air would stop all that.'

Madame Menton put the finishing touches to the room she had been tidying, re-arranging a large bowl of flowers on the table by the window. Ann had not noticed them before.

'Aren't they beautiful! Who are they from?' she asked.

Madame gave an imperceptible shrug of her shoulders.

'They arrived without a card,' she said truthfully.

For a moment, a deep pink coloured Ann's pale cheeks. She guessed at once they were from Paul.

'Oh, well!' she said casually. 'It was very kind of whoever sent them. It's most kind of you, too, to look after me this way, Madame. I'm sorry to be such a nuisance.'

'In a few days you will be quite well again,' Madame told her. 'I have

239

telephoned each evening to your mother who was much concerned about you. Which brings to my mind there are some letters for you which you have not been well enough to read until now. I will bring them to you.'

Only after Madame had returned with the letters and departed again to leave her in peace to read her mail, did Ann realise that although Monsieur Menton had sent his best wishes and promised to call in to see her after lunch, there had been no message from Luc. Perhaps, she thought, he would look in later.

She settled back to read her letters. There was one from James, filled with a glowing description of Pierre Menton; one from her father giving her the day to day family news, and the expected reply to hers from her mother.

Darling Ann,

I am writing back to you by return of post as you asked although I would have liked a little more time to think this problem over. Of course, darling, I trust you, but I cannot believe Madame Menton would have stopped you seeing this man, Paul, without good reason.

You say that he is a good deal older than you—thirty-three, in fact. That does seem a very large gap in your comparative ages and one that could have dangers you are not yet experienced enough to realise. You say he is unmarried and very attractive so I take it that there have been other women in his past, in which case he will be considerably more experienced in life than you are. Could it be that Madame Menton is afraid he will use this experience to make himself attractive to you without you quite realising what is happening? Since it is obviously very important to you that I give my permission for you to go out with him, I have to assume that you are already quite a little bit attracted!

It is difficult for me to come to a decision without knowing the man in question and without the chance to talk it all over with you, Ann. All I think I can say is that you are past the age where I would feel justified in forbidding you to make your own friends where you please and yet at the same time, my instinct tells me to accept Madame Menton's judgement in this. She is, after all, also a mother!

I think, darling, that this is a decision you must make for yourself. You will know in your own heart whether I would like this Paul or not, approve of him as a companion for you or not. You will know whether Daddy and James and I would like him and accept him here at home. If you have the slightest doubt in your mind, then be sensible and don't see any more of him than you can help. I quite see that in a small place you are likely to run into him from time to time but this is surely a little different from deliberately cultivating his society and encouraging his interest in you.

So I'm putting the ball back into your own court and by all means show this letter to Madame Menton should you decide Paul is above board and we'd all like and approve of him...

The rest of the letter referred in the main to the activities of the two boys and to saying what a nice child Pierre Menton had turned out to be.

...If his brother, Luc, is even half as nice, I wonder that you have time for Paul Duret. You spoke in such glowing terms of Luc your first week out there. Have you turned against him for some reason? Daddy and I quite thought there was a real friendship developing...

242

Ann put down the letter and lay back against her pillow. She was upset by it. She had hoped her mother would give an unqualified and definite opinion. It would have helped her to make up her own mind about Paul. As it was, she simply couldn't decide if he were really the dangerous seducer Luc had tried to paint him, or a misunderstood, sincere man who really meant it when he told her he was falling in love with her!

She tried to recall the events of the afternoon at Merveille. But try as she could, she could not manage to bring back any feeling of happiness or gaiety. She could only remember being slightly afraid of Paul and the nearness of her own submission to desire. And she wasn't even sure now if this were part of her nightmare dreams whilst she had been ill, or if it were reality.

She was further upset by the memory of Luc finding her there on the mountain in Paul's arms, drunk! She felt a little sick and very ashamed at the memory. How he must despise her! Yet he had cared enough about her to come looking for her! And to frog-march her home like a naughty little girl. He must have cared enough, too, to keep the truth from his mother, for there had been no mention by Madame Menton of her going out alone with Paul, or of her drinking too much wine. She wondered what Luc had told her and wished he would come and put her in the picture.

But the day wore on and still Luc did not appear at her door. Madame came with lunch. Later Monsieur Menton came and sat by the window and joked with her. Around seven o'clock, there were footsteps outside on the landing and Ann, waiting hopefully, was disappointed once more to see it was only Madame again, this time with her supper.

It was on the tip of her tongue to ask Madame if Luc would be coming in to see her, but her pride would not allow it. Luc was obviously furious with her. If this was his way of showing it, let him do so. She wasn't going to let him know she cared what he thought of her.

But her illness, combined with the heavy dosage of anti-biotics had depressed her more than she realised and she ended the day crying herself to sleep. Not the least cause of her tears were the comments in her mother's letter.

...you will know in your own heart, whether Daddy and I would like Paul and accept him here at home...

No, they would not like him. She knew that her father would certainly consider him far too old for her. James would call him 'a smoothy' and Mother wouldn't trust him any more than Madame Menton, even without knowing his reputation.

'I don't care what they'd all think of him!' she wept into her pillow. *'I like him.'*

But did she? She was no longer even sure if she did.

There was still no visit from Luc the following day. There were calls from the doctor and Monsieur Menton and Madame came at frequent intervals. But of Luc there was no sign.

In the afternoon there was an unexpected visit from Marie.

'Well, well, well!' she said as she came into the room with new copies of *Nova* and *Elle* which she planted on the bed. 'I see you are recovering, Ann? I also think I perhaps under-rated you a little. You certainly chose an excellent moment to be ill!'

Ann flushed.

'I didn't *choose* to be ill!' she said, and less defiantly: 'Thanks for the magazines. It was kind of you.'

Marie brushed the dark hair out of her eyes and sat down by the window.

'I thought you might be pleased to see me,' she said. 'You see, I am playing Cupid. I have brought you a letter.'

Again Ann blushed.

'Paul asked me to hand it to you personally and in private. Mission completed!'

She gave a short laugh as she threw a letter down on to the bed.

'I must admit I was in two minds whether or not to bring it. Luc would probably kill me if he knew. On the other hand, Paul threatened to storm the house and demand to see you if I did not. So of the two alternatives, I thought it might be less embarrassing all round if I delivered the goods myself. Go ahead—read it. I won't ask to share the contents.'

With a strange reluctance, Ann obediently slit open the envelope. The handwriting, thin, backward slanting, in French script, was difficult for her to decipher at first.

My dearest Ann,

You have so much to forgive me I hardly feel I dare ask forgiveness. I do so only because I have the very best of excuses for my behaviour—I love you. I never thought it possible that I should love a woman as I love you, my little one. I meant what I said at Merveille. I want to marry you. I would be the most proud man in the world if you would consent to be my wife.

Many people will try to deter you from marriage to a man such as I. I know I have not led a good life and have not much to offer you but love. But for you I will reform utterly. I will give up everything I have and start my life again for you. I can no longer conceive of any happiness in a life that does not include you. This you must believe, Ann.

Marie has been keeping me informed of your health. I have been tormented also because I cannot come to visit you. I doubt if that angry young man, Luc, would let me pass the door! I hope you received my flowers and understand that with them I was sending all my love.

I beg of you, from pity if not from love, to send me a message by Marie, telling her you have forgiven me for permitting you to

247

*over-drink the wine. Also for putting you in
the unhappy position where we had both to
lose our dignity in front of others. I had hoped
we would be quite uninterrupted and yet I can
find it in my heart to forgive Marie, who will
bring you this letter, as I hope you will find
it in your heart to forgive me.*

Your loving and desperate,
Paul

'Oh, dear!' Ann said involuntary.

Marie looked up in surprise.

'Sounds as if you're not exactly overjoyed
with your missive.'

Ann gave a deep sigh.

'Paul keeps on about me "forgiving
him"!' she said. 'I don't see what I'm
supposed to forgive him for. He didn't
force me to drink all that wine. I didn't
much like it at first but after a glass or two,
I was the one who wanted to finish it.'

Marie looked at Ann speculatively.

'Perhaps there was something else he did
for which he wants to be forgiven?'

'Well, what?' Ann said innocently. The
look on Marie's face brought the colour
back to her own. 'That's horrible!' she said.
'Of course nothing like that happened.'

'Well, that's a relief!' Marie said flatly.

Suddenly she smiled. 'I'm sure Luc as well as I thought the worst.'

'Luc?' Ann echoed. 'How *could* he?'

Marie raised her eyebrows.

'Was it really so impossible a thing to have happened, Ann? Be honest, if not with others at least with yourself. Paul is very attractive. He can be most persuasive. Was there honestly not one moment when you might have been tempted?'

The look on Ann's face answered her. More gently, Marie said:

'We are all human, Ann. We all have such moments, and men like Paul are able to create them more or less at will.'

'You and Luc and Madame Menton—you all want to make him out so beastly!' Ann cried. 'He isn't like that. He loves me!'

Marie shrugged.

'I know Paul, Ann, even if I do not know you. I will accept that he loves you, curious though it is to see Paul Duret finally caught in the web himself after all these years! I will even accept that he has not been "beastly" to you. But believe me—and I do know what I'm talking about—Paul has used women all his life. He doesn't really care about their feelings. Even now, when you wish to whitewash him—to make him out a reformed character—ask yourself what is he doing to Yvonne Verdos?'

'Madame Verdos?' Ann repeated. 'What has she to do with this?'

'Oh, Ann, you cannot be so ignorant!' Marie said. 'You must know she is his mistress?'

'That isn't true—not any more!' Ann argued.

'Because Paul said it was not so, you believe him? You really are a little innocent, Ann, after all. Imagine for yourself whether a man, living in the same house with a woman who was his mistress, ending the affair and remaining under her roof? Of course not! The woman herself would not permit it even if such an arrangement were agreeable to the man. Of course he still sleeps with her.'

'But he can't!' Ann cried. 'He's in love with me. He said so.'

Marie looked at her pityingly.

'It is really time you grew up, Ann. For men like Paul, there are the practicalities of life and there is love. They are separate and have different compartments. He may love you as you say, but he has "loved" other women. But Madame Verdos supports him, gives him the roof over his head and the money in his pocket. That is a practical matter.'

'But he said he wanted to marry me!' Ann whispered.

'So well he might. He may even mean it. But he will not bite the hand that feeds him until he is sure of you, Ann. Of that I have not the slightest doubt. I would believe more in Paul's protestations of love if he had walked out on Yvonne. Yet they were dancing together at the club last night, seemingly as devoted as ever.'

'I don't believe it!' Ann said. 'No one could be as two-faced as that. If you love someone, you don't want anyone else. He...he couldn't!' she ended feebly.

'Most men, no. Paul, yes! Though heaven knows why I am talking to you this way. It would suit me if you married Paul, and Luc forgot your existence.'

It was Ann's turn to laugh, but she did so with bitterness.

'You don't have to worry about *me*,' she said. 'Luc has forgotten my existence. He hasn't been to see me once. As far as I know, he hasn't even asked after me. No, Luc hates me now. You've certainly no cause to be jealous of the way he feels about me, Marie.'

Marie looked down at her fingernails, studying them as if they were of the greatest importance to her. She knew that what Ann said was not true. She had run into Luc several times in these last few days and when she had enquired after Ann, he had sounded deeply concerned about her health. He'd looked tired and unhappy. She'd tried to draw him out—to discover what was happening but he had refused to talk about Ann.

'Oh, he'll snap out of it in a day or two,' she said cheerfully. 'Luc doesn't bear grudges for long. If he was annoyed and upset by what happened, it'll wear off in time. Anyway, why should you care?'

'Because I like Luc—or I did!' Ann said darkly. 'Now I'm not sure. None of it was his business anyway. I think he just wanted to make a scene with Paul. I know he never liked him. I think I was just an excuse for him to pick a quarrel with Paul.'

Marie stood up.

'Well, as long as that's the way you see Luc, I can see I needn't worry,' she said airily. 'You know your trouble, don't you, Ann? You think everything should always be just the way you want it. Well, life isn't like that. It's ups and downs, good days and bad days, laughter and tears. There is a French proverb which says...'

'I know,' Ann interrupted, attempting to smile. *'Qui rit Vendredi, Dimanche pleurera!'*

Marie looked surprised.

'Fancy you knowing that!' she said. 'Well, I'll report back to Paul. No letter?'

Ann hesitated.

'No!' she said at last. 'No, I don't want to write to him.'

'No message then? No violent reciprocation of love?'

'I have never said I loved him. And if what you say is true about him and Madame Verdos...'

'Your ideals are shattered? Well, Paul won't thank me for that, though I spoke the truth, Ann, palatable or otherwise. I'll tell Paul you're thinking it all over. Meanwhile, keep smiling and get better soon.'

But events had been too much for Ann to follow Marie's advice. The tears that followed her departure sent her temperature up and that evening the doctor called for a second time and informed the worried Mentons that Ann had had a relapse.

14

Ann's temperature once more rose to 104. She was only half aware of what was going on around her. She heard Madame and the doctor mention some new antibiotic. There was talk of a tonsillectomy in the hospital in the valley. But she felt too ill and feverish to concern herself with the vague background murmuring.

It was a full two days before she began to respond to the changed drugs and then her slow convalescence began. Madame informed her that the doctor had feared at one stage she had a touch of pneumonia. Now, however, she was making satisfactory progress and it remained to see whether the infection in her throat would clear completely or if she would have to have her tonsils out.

'Oh, no!' Ann said weakly. 'Not at my age!'

But as Madame pointed out with amusement, tonsils were not like getting chickenpox or the measles. One could suffer equally as an adult or a child.

She was sitting in her now customary chair by the window, knitting. She turned a row of the heavy-knit blue polo-necked jersey she was making for Luc. Watching her, Ann saw with surprise how the garment had grown since she had last noticed it. Madame must have spent a lot of time here.

'You've been so good to me!' she said, speaking with difficulty because of the soreness of her throat. 'My mother couldn't have done more.'

Madame smiled. The click of the knitting needles was strangely comforting.

'Nevertheless, I am sure you would be happy to see your mother, no?'

Ann sighed.

'It does seem an extraordinary long time since I left home. So much seems to have happened. Mother and my home seem a very long way away.'

Madame nodded, still smiling.

'How is everyone?' Ann asked after a moment of silence. 'Monsieur Menton?'

'He is well—much concerned about you. You have become like a little daughter to him. He will visit you later this afternoon.'

Still no word from Luc? Ann thought

miserably. He must still be very angry with her. But at least, seeing how ill she had been, he might have forgotten his grievances sufficiently to send her a message.

'How is Luc?' she asked at last.

Madame did not look up from her knitting.

'He is well, too. He has gone to Geneva today.'

'To Geneva!' Ann cried. 'For good, you mean?'

'Oh, no. He will be back this evening.'

Madame did not volunteer any further information and Ann could not bring herself to ask for it. She felt weak and tired and before long, she had dozed off to the regular background click of Madame Menton's knitting needles.

When she woke it was dark. The room was empty and Madame had gone. Ann struggled into a sitting position and drank a little of the lime juice in the glass beside her bed. Her hand looked very white and thin and she thought:

'I really have been ill!'

No doubt it accounted for her deep depression. There did not seem anything to be happy about at the moment. It could certainly be some time before she was well and strong enough to go ski-ing again. She and Luc had quarrelled—irredeemably, it seemed. And now, on top of all that, she might possibly have to have her tonsils out in a strange hospital far from home.

Tears of self-pity trickled down her cheeks. She wished Madame would come back. She wished she were not quite alone. She thought of Paul but this only made her feel more miserable. She began to recall everything Marie had said about him and knew that although she did not want to, she believed Marie. Now the memory of her own behaviour with Paul sickened her as it must have sickened Luc. She wondered how Madame could still bring herself to be so nice to her!

There was a knock on the door and Madame came in with a visitor and a tray of lemon tea.

'Please do not stay too long, Madame Verdos,' Madame said as she switched on the light. 'Ann is still not at all well and talking tires her.'

'I'll be a few minutes only!'

Ann looked at the woman whom she now knew to be Paul's mistress. She half expected to be repelled by her but instead,' saw a very attractive, beautifully dressed woman with grey hair fashionably styled and large, dark grey eyes which were now regarding her with a long sympathetic look.

Madame showed the visitor to her own chair by the window, handed Ann her glass of hot tea and left the room. Her face looked stern and unsmiling as she left. Obviously, Madame Verdos's visit was unexpected and unwelcome.

'You must forgive me for this intrusion,' Yvonne Verdos said in that soft, husky voice of hers. 'I know you have been very ill but it is imperative I should talk to you.'

Her English was nearly perfect. Ann was grateful that she need not struggle to reply in French. She felt nervous and embarrassed although so far the older woman had seemed friendly and kind.

'You must not try to make replies,' said Yvonne gently. 'Madame Menton tells me your throat is painful, so I will do the talking if you are agreeable?'

Ann nodded, only just managing to conceal a sigh of relief.

'I have come to see you, of course, about Paul.' Now Yvonne was not looking at Ann but staring out of the window into the street. 'I have never done such a thing as this before. Always in the past I have ignored it when Paul has been...unfaithful.' She hesitated a moment and then went on quickly. '...but this is different. You see, I have not come on my behalf. I have come on Paul's. He loves you very much—as much as Paul is capable of loving anyone. No, do not try to talk,' she said as Ann tried to break in. 'Let me finish.'

She paused for only a moment before she went on:

'This is the first time Paul has been in love. He is suffering very much. He has begged me to release him from his obligations to me so that he can be free to marry you. This is how I know this time he is sincere. Marriage to Paul could change him, Mademoiselle Elgar. A man needs someone in his life whom he respects, worships a little. He cannot fully realise himself unless he is taxed a little to live up to an ideal. You are his ideal and you could make him happy.'

'But, Madame Verdos...' Ann broke in urgently. 'You don't understand. I...'

'Oh, I know very well that this might not be an excellent marriage for you. Paul has no estates, no family background. But he will not be without wealth to offer you. I will settle a sum of money on him on which you can both live very comfortably anywhere in the world. There would be no strings attached. I would not expect any part in your lives nor wish for any expressions of gratitude.'

'Madame, I must interrupt you!' Ann cried, deeply upset by this statement. 'You mustn't go on talking like that. I'd no idea—*no idea,*' she repeated, 'how much you must love him. I know what he has been to you. I don't understand how it's possible if you love him so much to be prepared to let him go!'

Yvonne's face was suddenly lined and etched with sadness.

'That is because you are young, my dear. You will learn that love is not taking—it is giving! And the truest test of all is giving up. I can give Paul up to you because I know you will make him happy in a way I never can, or ever could.'

'But I don't love him!' The words were out at last and hung between them as if they were tangible objects suspended in space.

Yvonne Verdos was staring at Ann now

with widened eyes and a look on her face which was half relief and half dismay.

'But Paul said he wanted to marry you!' For the first time, Ann heard uncertainty in the older woman's voice. Gently, she replied:

'He told me, too, that he wanted to marry me, but Madame, I have never even told Paul I loved him. As for marriage, such a thing never entered my head seriously. I don't want to get married for ages and ages—not to anyone. I've not so long left school and I haven't the slightest wish to settle down. I just don't know how things have happened the way they have—as if life out here has been accelerated to a speed I can't cope with.'

Yvonne Verdos drew a long sigh.

'At last I am beginning to understand a little. It is Paul, not you, who has brought this about. Mademoiselle, you are quite sure...that you do not love him?'

Although Ann had not known she was going to say so, she replied with complete conviction:

'Quite sure, Madame. I think he is attractive and charming and I enjoyed his company but love did not enter into it. I have never been in love—with anyone.'

She really did have no doubt about it now. Something in the conversation had convinced her that she was very far indeed from knowing what love was about. She could imagine only too well what it must have cost this beautiful, proud woman to come to her to plead for Paul, ready to destroy herself to make him happy. This was love and Paul must be cruel and stupid to think of leaving her.

'But you have not said all this—to Paul?' Yvonne was asking her.

Ann shook her head.

'There hasn't really been a chance.'

'He is tormented by anxiety!' Yvonne said. 'He neither eats nor sleeps and I know it is because of you. He could not prevent himself from talking about you.'

'Well, I'm quite willing to write and tell him how I feel,' Ann said. 'The sooner he forgets about me the better. Really, I'm not worth all the trouble, Madame. I know that. I'm not...not worth liking, even. I'm frivolous and shallow and...'

'And not at all well yet!' Yvonne said, rising to her feet. 'It is natural you should be depressed and I feel guilty that I have tired you. Nevertheless, I am glad I came. I thought it would be very difficult talking to you. If, when you feel a little stronger, you would write to Paul? The sooner he knows it is all useless, the sooner he will begin to recover.'

'I'll write now. You can take the letter!' Ann said, but Yvonne shook her head.

'Then Paul will know I have seen you and will think I tried to set you against him—and succeeded. No, it must come from you without my knowledge, Mademoiselle.'

And at least she could help Yvonne Verdos this much, Ann thought as the older woman left the room. Paul would never know from her that she had been to visit her.

She felt infinitely sorry for the older woman—and awed by the enormity of a love which could bring such self-sacrifice. Now, for the rest of her life, she would have this knowledge as a yardstick. It was easy to take from love; harder to give and hardest of all to give up. When she was ready to give up her own happiness for someone else's, she would know she was really in love.

Surprisingly, she felt relaxed and almost happy after Madame Verdos's departure. She slept once more and woke refreshed as Madame Menton came into the room.

'Well, my dear,' she said, straightening Ann's bed cover and plumping up her pillow. 'You have a little surprise—or perhaps I should say, a big one. Here is your dear Mama to see you.'

For one brief moment, Ann had imagined she was going to announce Luc. Just for an instant, she felt a pang of disappointment and then the real, genuine happiness at seeing her mother flooded over her as Mrs Elgar came into the room and enveloped her in a warm loving embrace.

'I can't believe it!' Ann said over and over again, hugging Mrs Elgar with as much strength as she could muster. 'I just can't believe it!'

'Well, I'm no ghost!' said Mrs Elgar laughing. She looked down at Ann comically. 'And I wish I could say the same of you. You've lost pounds and pounds, Ann.'

It was some time before the flow of conversation stopped and Ann could ask:

'But why did you come all this way, Mother? I'm getting better, not worse!'

'I know, darling, but we've got to come to a decision about these wretched tonsils

265

of yours. Daddy thought it would be a good idea if I came and sorted everything out and checked up on you at the same time. We really were a little bit disturbed by your last letter, you know.'

Ann's face coloured.

'You needn't have been.' She changed the conversation. 'How did you come? Did you fly? Did you take the train from Geneva?'

Suddenly, she recalled Madame Menton telling her Luc had gone to Geneva for the day.

'Luc went to meet you, didn't he?' she asked in a strange, stiff little voice.

Her mother nodded.

'What a nice boy he is, Ann. We had a lovely long chat in the train. So sensible and very like his young brother. And, darling, I won't have you blaming Luc for what I'm going to say. What he told me was entirely for your good and it would be very unfair if you were to feel he had been telling tales. I was determined to find out what Madame Menton had against this man you're in love with and if he hadn't told me, I'd have made Madame herself do so. So I forced Luc's confidence. You do understand?'

Ann let go her breath. She had followed this long statement with difficulty but she gathered enough from it to realise that Luc had told her mother all about Paul. What she did not understand was her mother's statement that Paul was the man she was 'in love with'.

'I'm not in love with Paul, Mother. Whatever made you think so? I'd have told you if I was, in my letter.'

Mrs Elgar looked vaguely relieved and not a little puzzled.

'Well, that's what I thought when I left England. But Luc himself told me you were in love with this Paul. He didn't seem to be in any doubt about it. He was so afraid you were seriously thinking of marrying him.'

Suddenly Ann started to laugh. It was a little hysterical and she forced herself to calm down.

'Well, really, it's almost too much!' she said. 'You're the second person today who's accused me of being in love with Paul. As to Luc—I can't think how he can think such a thing.'

Mrs Elgar gave Ann a shrewd glance.

'From what I gathered, you yourself told Luc, on your way down the mountain, that you would marry Paul just as soon as you felt like it. I think those were the words he used. He said you told him that in a cable car coming back from a place called Merveille.'

'Well, I was very tight then!' Ann said. 'I can't be sure if I said that or not. I do vaguely remember having an argument with him about Paul and telling Luc I'd do what I wanted and wasn't going to have him tell me what to do!'

Mrs Elgar gave Ann a worried glance.

'Darling, do you know what you just said? That you were tight? I presume you meant it. Just what has been going on?'

So Ann started at the beginning. She left out nothing—not even the details of Yvonne Verdos's visit earlier in the day. Finally, she said:

'So you see, Mother, I've behaved pretty badly to everyone and now Luc hates me and I've hurt Madame Verdos and Paul and I'm beginning to wish I'd never, ever come to Aiguille!'

'And that, at least, isn't true!' said Mrs Elgar smiling. 'You know very well that up to the time everything started to go wrong, you were loving every minute of it, including wrapping two young men around your little finger.'

Ann's cheeks now were a deep pink.

'But that isn't fair, Mother. I wasn't trying to play Luc against Paul or vice versa.'

'Well, by the sound of it, you weren't making a bad attempt!' Mrs Elgar said unsympathetically. 'Frankly, darling, I think it's high time you gave a little more thought to other people. You can't be a butterfly and flit through sunshine all your life. And there's a big difference, you know, between boys and young men like Luc Menton. At Luc's age, you can be very, very hurt.'

'I didn't mean to hurt him!' Ann cried. 'I honestly didn't mean it, Mother. I like Luc. I've liked him all along. If it hadn't been for Paul, I might even have...'

'Fallen in love with him?' Mrs Elgar asked gently.

'Well, it doesn't matter now. Luc hates me and I expect he always will. And I don't care. If he'd really loved me even a little, he'd have come to see me, told me we were still friends.'

'Oh, Ann,' said Mrs Elgar. 'No wonder Madame Menton said on the telephone that she thought "my little girl" might like to see me. You must grow up, darling, and stop feeling so aggrieved every time you don't get your own way. Think of what Luc must be feeling and use some of your self-pity on him. It must be very disillusioning for him to find out what kind of a girl you really are.'

'You make me sound horrible!' Ann said miserably. 'I didn't mean to hurt him. I knew he liked me but...'

'...but that wasn't going to stop your flirtation with Paul, was it? Obviously Luc's feelings weren't very important to you so you've no right to complain if yours aren't very important to him now.'

'Yes, I know, but he could at least come and see me once!' Ann cried.

'Maybe he will. Now, darling, I think that's enough talking. You've almost lost your voice. I'm going down to have a chat with that nice Madame Menton, then I'll bring up your supper and come and sit with you. How will that be?'

'Nice!' whispered Ann. Her pride would not allow her to add: 'And please bring Luc!'

15

Mrs Elgar remained three days. During that time, Ann's health improved rapidly but the doctor, in whom everyone seemed to have great faith, was convinced the infected tonsils should be removed as soon as Ann had regained a little more strength.

'We could fly you home, darling!' Mrs Elgar told Ann. 'But I think this would be rather expensive on top of my fare out here. Would you feel very miserable having those wretched tonsils out in the hospital in the valley? Madame Menton tells me it is very modern and that the Swiss surgeons are excellent.'

'I wouldn't mind!' Ann said. 'But won't the operation be expensive? At home I could be done on National Health.'

'Well, fortunately Daddy has a medical insurance and so your expenses will be covered by them,' Mrs Elgar told her.

Ann was silent. In one way, she wished she could go home and stay home. It was all very well whilst she was lying here in the privacy of her bedroom but as soon as she was fit again, she would have to get up and face the world and she really didn't feel up to it. There would be no avoiding Paul and that was going to be difficult and embarrassing. He had not replied to her letter and she couldn't know whether he was hurt or furious or if he had been reconciled with Madame Verdos. She hoped he had. She had liked the older woman and felt a deep pity mixed with admiration for her. But she did not want to meet her, either.

Then of course, there was Luc. He had still not been near her, sent any message or good wishes for her recovery.

Infuriatingly neither her mother nor Madame Menton, nor even Monsieur, mentioned Luc when they were with her and she could not bring herself to ask about him. She was not quite convinced that he had finished with her and this was going to be more than awkward when she was up and about again.

'I suppose I couldn't come home and *stay* home?' she asked her mother tentatively.

Mrs Elgar gave Ann a quick searching glance.

'Are you sure that's what you want, Ann, or are you just wanting to run away from your problems?'

Ann blushed. Trust her mother to get to the root of the matter.

'I thought that might be it!' said Mrs Elgar gently. 'Well, running away won't solve anything, Ann. If you've started off your year in Aiguille on the wrong foot, you should stick it out and make the very best of the time left to you. If it's any encouragement to you, you might be relieved to hear that your friend Paul Duret has returned to Paris with Madame Verdos.'

Ann's eyes widened.

'Are you sure?' she asked.

'Quite sure. Madame Menton herself told me. So you see, there will not be any awkwardness there.'

Ann sighed. In a way, Paul had been the least of her worries. It was going to be so much harder facing Luc, knowing how he despised her.

'By the way,' Mrs Elgar went on casually. 'I gather that Luc is thinking of starting work in Geneva earlier than he had intended. He may go down there next week.'

Ignoring Ann's little gasp of surprise, she went on:

'He and his father were discussing it last night. Luc seemed very anxious to make a start on his new job. Monsieur Menton thought the office would be quite prepared to take him on earlier than originally planned.'

Ann drew a deep sigh. It was hardly surprising, although the news had shocked her. Obviously Luc was anxious to get away from her.

'Is it...because of me?' she asked miserably.

'Perhaps! Nothing was said about you, of course, but I have the impression Luc was beginning to get very fond of you, Ann. Maybe he feels it would be best all round if he removes himself to a safe distance.'

'You mean, he is running away from me?' Ann asked. 'I thought you said running away didn't solve anything.'

'Well, there's nothing for Luc to solve, is there? I expect he just wants to avoid any embarrassment to you.'

Ann's mouth tightened.

'Why should I be embarrassed?' she asked defiantly. 'I don't see what this has to do with me.'

'That's all right then. You can forget about it,' Mrs Elgar said, the faintest tinge of amusement escaping Ann's notice, so disconcerted was she. 'Now, shall we reach a decision about the hospital, darling? It's agreed you'll have the tonsils out here as soon as the doctor says you're well enough?'

'I suppose so!' Ann agreed. But she no longer had the slightest wish to stay in Aiguille. Only pride forbade her begging her mother to let her go home.

Ann was allowed up the day her mother left. She was sitting in the window-chair, feeling weak and shaky, when Mrs Elgar came in to say goodbye.

'I'll be leaving in about half an hour,' she said. 'Luc is taking me to the airport which is very kind of him. Then he'll remain in Geneva and start work on Monday.'

Ann's heart sank. So it was all arranged. In a little while, Luc would be gone and she wouldn't even be able to hope any longer that he would forgive her and pay her a visit.

Tears sprang to her eyes and she turned her head swiftly away so that her mother should not see them.

'I don't care!' she told herself. 'Luc isn't important. I'm only upset because Mother is leaving.'

'I'll just finish my last-minute packing and then I'll be back to say a final goodbye,' said Mrs Elgar. If she had noticed Ann's tears, she did not refer to them. As the door closed behind her, Ann allowed herself the luxury of a good weep. She was dabbing at her eyes when the door opened again. Keeping her head turned away, she sniffed and said:

'Packing finished, Mother?'

'All complete!' But it was not her mother's voice. It was Luc's. Ann forgot her swollen eyes and swung round to stare at him. He smiled at her in the old, friendly way.

'Well, I'm glad to see you better!' he lied, secretly aghast at her pallor and the thinness of her face. 'It was bad luck becoming ill in this way.'

His kind voice and sympathetic manner when she had expected him to be cold and distant, weakened Ann's already flagging spirits. The tears began to flow again.

'Oh, Ann, don't cry, please!' Suddenly Luc was kneeling on the floor in front of her chair, his hand gently trying to wipe away the tears with a large white handkerchief.

'I c-c-can't help it!' Ann said. 'I'm...s-so...miserable!'

Luc smiled tenderly.

'You are upset because your nice Mama is departing. But you will feel happier when you are quite well again. Remember, you were not in the least homesick when you arrived from England. You cannot have forgotten how happy you were in Aiguille?'

Ann tried to smile.

'Yes, I know—the sun and snow and ski-ing and everything!' Suddenly she realised that the end had come for her ski-ing lessons with Luc.

'Now I'll never be good enough to come down from the Point!' she wailed.

'But of course you will!' Luc said firmly, though his eyes looked wretched and his voice was stiff with controlled emotions. He had meant to come and say only the most formal of farewells. He would really have preferred not to see Ann again but his mother had insisted he must observe at least the courtesies and Mrs Elgar had insisted that Ann would be heartbroken if he didn't say goodbye.

In fact, he knew very well that Ann didn't care whether he left or not. He meant nothing at all to her and feeling as he did about her, he knew he could not go on seeing her day after day, his love growing deeper and stronger and harder than ever to hide. He had been afraid to see her knowing that he as yet still had very little control over himself and might well reveal his love again by a look or a gesture.

But the sight of Ann, so pale and thin and unhappy, was making it impossible for him to stay cold and remote.

'You will find an excellent ski-instructor who will give you much better lessons than I,' he said. 'I am not really a good teacher.'

'Oh, but you were,' Ann cried. 'And it was all such fun, Luc. I can't bear the thought of you going away!'

The words were out before she could stop them. She heard her own voice with a sense of shock. She had not realised it until she had spoken aloud, but they were true. She couldn't bear the thought of him leaving.

'I have to go!' Luc said in a small hard voice. He was nearly at breaking point.

Couldn't she see how her words hurt him? She merely wanted his friendship and he couldn't give it to her without love.

'But why?' Ann asked. 'Is it because you don't like me any more?' Without waiting for an answer, she went on abjectly: 'I don't blame you for hating me!'

'Hating you?' Now Luc lost the last vestige of self-control. 'Don't you understand, Ann? I love you. I love you. It is because I love you I must go. Maman understands. Perhaps your mother also. They know it is impossible for me to live here. I could not hide my love for you and it would make you miserable.'

Ann discovered she was holding her breath. She let it out now in a long sigh. She couldn't begin to sort out all the conflicting emotions Luc's declaration had aroused. She could think only of her own intense happiness that Luc did not, after all, hate her. He loved her—loved her the way Madame Verdos had described it. He had been prepared to give up his own pleasure in being at home in order to save her embarrassment. But it wouldn't be an embarrassment, she thought wildly. She was glad Luc loved her. She wanted him to love her.

She stared at him, confused, wide-eyed, questioning.

'Why didn't you come to see me?' she asked. 'I wanted so much to see you, Luc. I wanted to ask you to forgive me for the way I behaved. I've been miserable thinking you were hating me all this time.'

'Oh, Ann!' Luc said on a little sigh. 'As if I could hate you for long. I didn't dare come. I was afraid of myself.'

Suddenly she smiled.

'I'm so glad you came just now!' she said honestly.

Luc's head shot up and he looked at her searchingly.

'But why, Ann? What should it matter so much to you?'

She took a deep breath.

'Because somehow it just does matter —very much,' she said slowly. 'I'm trying to be perfectly honest, Luc. I don't really understand why I feel so happy but I know it is because you said you loved me. I think it is possible after all, I am in love with you!'

She smiled at him shyly.

'All the time I've been lying here ill, I've thought about little else but you and how unhappy I was because you didn't care any longer whether I lived or died! Luc, I don't know if I know what real love is. Perhaps Mother is right and I badly need to grow up a little. In a funny sort of way, I think I have grown up a lot this last week. I've begun to get my values straight and all I do know is that...that I value the way you feel about me. It's more important to me than anything else. Is that love?'

He reached out his arms and drew her to him. His eyes were full of tenderness and a new hope.

'I don't know,' he said. 'I don't think it matters if it is love or only the beginning of love. That is more than enough for me. I can wait while you do your growing up. I can wait weeks and months and years, if necessary.'

Suddenly he was kissing her. Her eyes closed and she let herself relax into the comfort of his embrace, wanting his kiss, returning it with a new strange feeling of tenderness. She felt very, very happy. As she drew away from him, she saw that Luc's face, always handsome, was filled with a kind of radiant joy.

'Oh, Luc!' she breathed, her heart thudding. 'Do you have to go to Geneva?

Must you really go away?'

For a moment his face clouded. Then he reached out a hand and said softly:

'I don't have to go any more, Ann, but I think it might still be a good plan if I do so. It will give you time to sort everything out. I don't want to confuse you and when I hold you in my arms and kiss you, I think we are both confused. When you tell me that you love me, I want to know that it is really so.'

'But, Luc...I shall miss you...terribly!' Ann said as he drew her back into his arms.

He smiled, happy again.

'I shall miss you. But I will come back at the weekends, Ann, and we shall ski together when you are well again and be very, very happy. I think I would prefer it should be this way. I want with all my heart to be here, near you, yet even more, I want to go away from you so that you may make up your mind how you feel without persuasion from me.'

She was on the point of arguing with him, but suddenly she realised that her own wishes were of secondary importance. Luc's happiness came first and if this was the way he wanted it, she wasn't going to make it harder for him by pleading with him to stay. She had no justification for doing so until she could be absolutely sure she did love him.

'Luc!' She smiled up at him. 'I once thought you were like a very, very nice older brother. I don't feel that way any more!'

He laughed.

'I never thought of you as a sister. I think I fell in love with you in the train bringing you here from Geneva. Oh, Ann, I wonder if you can understand how truly happy I am to know that at least my love is not unwelcome to you; that there is even a hope you care a little, too.'

'A little!' Ann repeated. 'It's far, far more than that.'

The door opened and Mrs Elgar came in. She looked at the two young people without surprise.

'So my instinct was right!' she said contentedly. 'I told you you mattered a great deal to her, Luc. But you wouldn't believe me!'

Luc stood up and smiled back at Ann's mother.

'She is your daughter so it is perhaps understandable that you know her better than I. Is it time we went, Madame?'

Mrs Elgar nodded regretfully.

'You'll take care of her when she goes into hospital I know,' Mrs Elgar said. 'So I shan't worry about her.'

She bent and kissed Ann goodbye. There were no tears now. Luc, too, kissed her, oblivious to her mother's presence.

'I will see you next weekend!' he promised. 'And looking much, much fitter, I hope.'

'I'll get better quickly now!' Ann said, knowing that the wanting to be better was half the battle. 'Goodbye, Luc!'

'No, *au revoir*,' he corrected her and gave her a last quick kiss.

Mrs Elgar stayed a moment longer.

'Happy darling?' she asked.

'Yes!' Ann said simply. 'Though I wish you weren't going,' she added.

'Nonsense!' laughed Mrs Elgar. 'You don't need me with a nice young man like Luc hovering over you. You do really like him, don't you, Ann? I wouldn't want to see him hurt.'

'I won't hurt him,' Ann said softly. 'And I do really like him...very, very much.'

'I'm glad!' said Mrs Elgar as she closed the door softly behind her. She was sure

that it wouldn't be long before that liking
changed to something more. It was exactly
the right way to fall in love.

The publishers hope that this book has given you enjoyable reading. Large Print Books are especially designed to be as easy to see and hold as possible. If you wish a complete list of our books, please ask at your local library or write directly to: Magna Large Print Books, Long Preston, North Yorkshire, BD23 4ND, England.

This Large Print Book for the Partially sighted, who cannot read normal print, is published under the auspices of

THE ULVERSCROFT FOUNDATION